Narrow Escape . . .

Suddenly, the coach was utterly dark, and Seldon realized, too late, what Strawn had been watching for. The railroad tunnel on this slope of the Hurumpaws! Strawn had planned well, for the impenetrable darkness of the tunnel was broken by the flame of a forty-five in the hand of Gary Strawn, and Seldon was thrust back hard against the seat by the smashing impact of the slug.

He lurched sideways, his move instinctive, and the bullet that might have split his heart smashed along his ribs. At first the pain and shock almost swept him into a greater darkness, but he fought for a tight hold on himself, and he struck out with his fist at the man across from him. But Strawn was already gone, lurching out into the aisle and along it toward the end of the coach. Seldon went stumbling after him, praying for strength, thinking, *I can't let him get away!*

Also by Norman A. Fox

Silent in the Saddle

NORMAN A. FOX

A DELL BOOK

Published by
Dell Publishing
a division of
Bantam Doubleday Dell Publishing Group, Inc.
666 Fifth Avenue
New York, New York 10103

The trademark Dell® is registered in the U.S. Patent and Trademark Office.

ISBN: 0-440-21053-4

Printed in the United States of America

Published simultaneously in Canada

November 1992

10 9 8 7 6 5 4 3 2 1

OPM

Contents

1 ⋮ A Six-Gun for Sale

He came to this Calumet as unobtrusively as a person of his appearance could, riding in at high noon and making his quiet way toward the largest livery stable. He'd paralleled the railroad in its wide swing through the sprawling Hurumpaw Hills, and he'd seen high country and flat country, crowded timber and grassy emptiness, all in the same day's riding, and now he had reached the hub of Hurumpaw Basin, this ungainly cowtown. Calumet was bleak and Calumet was ugly; and if it seethed today with a restless, surging excitement, the stranger showed no interest in the sundry manifestations of that excitement.

Dismounting before the livery, he rooted the hostler out of the coolest shadows, jerked his thumb at the rangy roan gelding he'd ridden, and said, "Give him the best," keeping his voice at a whisper, not in the manner of a man with a secret, but in the way of one who speaks softly from long habit.

"Sure," said the hostler and took his look at the stranger's saddle with its double cinch and its horn that was built for trying instead of dallying. "Texan, eh?" he surmised. "Riding through?"

But the stranger was already striding out of the stable, and he came to the edge of the boardwalk and stood there, making a high, fine figure and a somber one. His spurs were of silver, and they'd been wrought in Old Mexico, and the sunlight danced upon them; his neckerchief, knotted tightly around his throat, was a wisp of flaming orange, but otherwise he wore black from his boots to his flat-crowned, stiff-brimmed sombrero. Even the foxing of his California pants and the buttons of his double-breasted shirt blended with his attire. He carried his gun lashed down against his right thigh—the holster was cut for quick work—and he looked like a man to whom a Colt was more than an ornament.

He had traveled far, this man; but he gave no sign that this was strange country to him, keeping the saturnine gravity of his high-boned face unchanged, and looking at Calumet with the steady-eyed look of one who knows no home and seeks none. From where he made his stand, he could see the straggly row of false-fronts that faced each other across the dusty width that was the street. Intermittently, cottonwoods reared themselves in gnarled splendor, and the breeze spoke sibilantly in their shimmering leaves. Anchoring the street was the rusty grandeur of the two-storied brick courthouse, and before it there were more wagons and hitched saddle horses than would have been usual on a weekday. All these things the stranger saw, seemingly taking no interest, and then he headed for the faded, garish sign of the Silverbow Hotel.

The Silverbow boasted a dining room, as its shingle proclaimed, but the stranger had to do some sidestepping before he reached it, bucking the restless flow of men along the boardwalks and matching curious stares with his own calm impassivity. He got under the wide wooden awning of the hotel and into the dining wing and found a table, and he whispered, "Steak and spuds," when a waitress finally wended her way to him. Eating slowly, he found what possessed this town, for the room was crowded and conversation boiled all around him.

"Hanging him tomorrow!" a man at the next table said. "You'd think Boaker might 'a' waited a couple of weeks. The whole thing was pretty fast business, if you ask me. It ain't ten days since Limpy was arrested, and here he's on his way to spoil a new rope."

"Judge Boaker's scared," his companion decided and

washed down his remark with a scalding draught of coffee. "So's Sheriff Endicott and Gary Strawn. I tell you it put feathers in a man's guts to sit there in court this morning and see Limpy shaking his fist and sayin' he'd live to see the judge, the sheriff, the deputies, and the county attorney doing an air dance. Damn it, I could almost believe he was likely to make his threat come true—jail, gallows, and guns, or not."

"No, I reckon Limpy McSwain's done his last killing," the other countered. "But Ord Wheeler and his Raggedy Pants boys are still in town, though Gus Banning took his S-5 crew and cleared out. Wheeler won't let Limpy be hung. I've got ten dollars that says there'll be trouble before the sun stands very high tomorrow."

All this the stranger heard, and more of the same; and when the time came he pushed back his plate, left silver money beside it, and strolled to the broad porch. There were chairs here and he chose one, crossing his long legs on the railing before him and lolling back in such a way as to favor his gun. And here he sat with half-lowered lids, watching the steady stream of traffic along the boardwalks, studying the various brands on the saddlers at the gnawed hitch rail before the Silverbow, and seeing other things as well. And he was this way when the sheriff came down the street and spoke to him.

"You're Hush Considine," said the sheriff.

This lawman of Hurumpaw County had a body too big for the short legs which supported it. Grown gray in the harness, the sheriff possessed that genial personality which ensures votes, but he had assumed a sober grimness for this moment's work. The stranger considered him and also considered the statement he had made. The stranger had spoken seven words since he'd come to Calumet; now he made his longest speech.

"Is being Hush Considine against Montana law, Sheriff?" he asked.

The sheriff—Endicott—frowned. "I spotted you the

minute you rode in," he said. "This may be a long way from the Big Bend country of Texas, but we hear things. It didn't take me long to recollect the description of a jigger who favors black and keeps his throat covered. You had your Adam's apple grazed by a bullet, didn't you, Considine? You don't talk above a whisper because it hurts you. Yeah, I know you, and I know your rep. I've got no legal claim on you. Nobody has. You sell your gun to the highest bidder, and you keep on the right side of the law. Now, just take it easy! Just to play safe, I posted one of my deputies on the roof of yonder store. And he's got a rifle lined on your brisket!"

The stranger yawned. "I know," he said. "I watched him climb up there. Clumsy fellow, isn't he?"

He was laughing with his eyes, and they were surprisingly blue. "Just what is it you're trying to get off that broad chest of yours, Sheriff?"

He could see that none of this was as Sheriff Endicott had planned it, and the breath went out of the lawman in an explosive gust, and Endicott blurted, "I need your gun, Considine. I'll pay fifty dollars for the use of it between now and high noon tomorrow."

"Shortage of guns in town, Sheriff?"

"Too many," Endicott snapped. "But they're all on one side of a fence or another. I need a straddler. Would you work for the law?" Suspicion drew his tufted eyebrows into one. "Or did you come here already hired out?"

"No, the For Sale sign is still hanging," the stranger said and gave a moment to some inward reflection. Uncrossing his legs, he came to a stand and vaulted over the railing to the sheriff's side. "Till noon tomorrow," he added. "Why not?"

Endicott sighed again, lifted his hand in a sheepish signal to the posted deputy on the roof beyond and said, "Come along to the courthouse. Judge Boaker will want to see you. It was his idea."

They went down the street side by side, Endicott taking two steps to the stranger's one; and in this manner they came to the brick building whose hitchrail was less cluttered now, and they climbed a wooden stairs that had been cupped by the passage of many feet. The way led along a hall that was dim and shadowy and musty with the years, and into a room oak-paneled and clinging to dignity like a tired old man with a stovepipe hat. A big window fronted on the street, and two men stood before it, the one, big-bodied and silver-haired, turning to say, "Ah, Sheriff. So you fetched him."

"Judge Boaker," Endicott said and nodded in the direction of the second man. "And Gary Strawn, our county attorney. Gents, this is Hush Considine."

"Mighty pleased," said the stranger. "How do I earn the fifty?"

He spoke in that lazy whisper of his, and from the look of him he might have been a man bored beyond any casual interest. But all the while he was inventorying these three, and his decision was that the real strength lay in Gary Strawn. The attorney was tall and he looked as though he might be made of steel. A fellow of indefinite age, his black hair had a sprinkling of gray, and his black mustache hid the fullness of his lip. He wore a dark business suit, but the trousers were tucked into hand-stitched boots that had been grooved by a stirrup's rub, and the gun-belt around Strawn's lean middle was limber with use.

Judge Boaker personified the law of the statute books to a far greater degree than Strawn. Boaker had a pink and placid face, and he smiled and said, "We have a dangerous situation to handle, Considine. This morning we concluded the trial of a certain Limpy McSwain, charged with the murder of Tom Muller, a cowhand employed by the S-5, the largest ranch in Hurumpaw Basin. McSwain was working for a group of smaller ranchers who call themselves the Raggedy Pants Pool. Our problem amounts to this: the Raggedy Pants boys may try to save their man from hanging. I set the execution for tomorrow morning to get it over with quickly. We'd be pleased to have your gun helping uphold the law meanwhile."

The stranger nodded. "I've heard the talk of this town," he said. "Let's get this straight. Am I to help keep McSwain from being broken out of jail—or am I to protect you three from McSwain?"

Anger brought a quick rush of color to Strawn's face. "So you know about that, eh?" he said. "Shucks, man, do you think we're a bunch of rabbits, hiding from the threat of a kill-crazy cripple who's as good as hanged? Yes, McSwain swore he'd see us all dangle. But in my years as a lawyer—and I've been one for more years than you've lived—I've been threatened hundreds of times. Your job is to see that the law is carried out as the court ordered it."

Footsteps echoed along the hallway, and a tall and cadaverous man with a deputy's badge upon his vest burst into the room. He said, "I talked with Ord Wheeler, Easy. I ordered him and his Raggedy Pants boys out of town. Ord did some grumbling, but I reckon he'll go."

"Good," Easy Endicott said. Then: "This is Hush Considine, Sid. Sid Greenleaf, my chief deputy. Considine's a special deputy till McSwain's hung." His glance shifted to the stranger. "That right?"

The stranger looked straight at Judge Boaker. "There's a saying in Texas," he observed. " 'When a man needs a gun, he needs it bad.' " He saw the way those words hit the silver-haired jurist, and then he added, "I'll be having a look for this Ord Wheeler—just to make sure he really understood what Greenleaf told him."

Strawn said, "That makes us beholden to you, Considine. Sorry I blew off. I just wanted you to understand that we aren't afraid of McSwain."

The stranger smiled. "I wonder," he said and left the room.

Outside the courthouse, he paused to fashion a smoke, teetering on the edge of the boardwalk and taking his time at the task. He stood there until the quirley had burned to his fingers; and he was stamping out the stub when a group of horsemen stirred the dust of the street, heading east, a dark-browed giant leading them, a boy in point of years yet with the mature gravity that comes from assuming responsibility. Many brands made up this loosely strung cavalcade, and the stranger guessed that this was Ord Wheeler and his Raggedy Pants Pool obeying the law's decree.

Taking a turn up the length of the boardwalk and crossing over and coming back again, he found that the town had settled to quietness in the hour since his coming. He retraced his steps to the hotel porch, found the same chair he'd occupied before, slumped into it, and seemed to doze. Yet all the while his eyes were on the courthouse door. He saw Easy Endicott waddle out, and Sid Greenleaf likewise make a departure, and after that the townsmen who passed by the hotel gave him long and speculative looks, and he knew now that the word had gone around about him.

Judge Boaker came out at last, frock-coated and carrying a silver-headed cane. The jurist moved along the hotel side of the street without breaking step until he stood below the stranger. Here Boaker fished into his coat for a cigar, and with it between his teeth, he said, "Do you have a match?"

The stranger supplied one; Boaker got it to blazing, and around his cupped hands he said, "Little cottage. White fence. Far end of the street. At dark."

The stranger's eyes gave silent agreement, and Boaker walked on. After that the stranger fell to dozing, the sun arced across the sky, poised on the pine-crested tops of the huddled hills to the west, and the shadows ran long and cool and purple.

Bestirring himself, the stranger went inside for his supper, lingering over it and letting the darkness gather. Out on the street again afterward, he sauntered along the boardwalk, passing the last of the stores and saloons and coming to a stretch of dwellings which he studied casually. Deepening dusk wove its smoky mist over the town, and he was abreast of one of the cottonwoods when a voice spoke from its shadows.

"Considine!" it said.

He leaped sideward, snapping out his gun at the same time; and that was pure reflex, for the one who'd spoken was a girl. He eased the iron back into leather and said, "Yes," peering all the while and trying to see her better. She'd come to the middle buttons on his shirt, he judged; and at first he had only a blurred impression of a white shirt and a dark, divided riding-skirt. But now he could see her heart-shaped face, beautiful with the untouched loveliness of blossoming womanhood, and her wealth of honey-colored hair; and he doffed his sombrero saying, "I'm sorry, miss."

Her words came then with a rush. "Would you like to make five hundred dollars?" she asked.

He let his first shock pass before he said, "How?"

"By letting Limpy McSwain out of jail. You could do it! I know you were made a special deputy today. Everybody knows it. Easy Endicott wanted the word to get around that he had a famous Texas gunhawk backing him. You could get into the jail, and you could get out again—with McSwain. Are you interested?"

"McSwain kin to you?"

The curl of her lip gave him answer.

"Friend, then?" he prodded.

"I hate him!" she snapped. "I hate him and all of his kill-crazy kind. But I want him out of jail. You work for the highest bidder, don't you? Will you do it?"

"Did McSwain really kill Tom Muller?"

"Of course he did!"

"Then I reckon we'll let the law take its course," he said.

"A thousand dollars?"

He shook his head. "No."

Her shoulders slumped, and he saw speech trembling on her lips. He was much closer to her now, and their eyes held, and she must have read some of his harsh and unyielding creed in the look of him. She said, "Very well, then. It was a good try. Would it be asking too much to have you forget you ever saw me?"

He let his eyes measure her again; and suddenly he smiled, and was younger. "It's asking an awful lot, miss," he said.

She colored quickly. "I didn't mean *that*. And you know it!"

His smile faded. "I never saw you," he said. "Five minutes from now, I'll probably be wondering if that isn't so anyway. Tell me, if I reached out and touched you, would you vanish?"

"Oh—!" she cried and faded into the shadows, and he heard the swift beat of her retreating boots. For a long time he stood looking in the direction she'd gone, still holding his sombrero in his hand. Then he shrugged and took up his search for the little cottage with the white fence that should be somewhere at this edge of town.

2 ⋮ Smoky Assignment

The house of Hiram Tomlinson Boaker stood apart from the town proper; and because it was a low, rambling cottage with its paint kept fresh and white, it stood apart also in appearance, a brave attempt at beauty in a land where the practical made for ugliness. There were flowers in the spacious yard, and a tree stood to the back of the building, and light from a bay window laid a warm and welcome splash across the veranda. The stranger, coming to the end of his quest, gave all this his consideration, then carefully avoided the light, skirting the cottage to its rear.

Here, beneath the tree's deepening shadow, he found Boaker. Wicker chairs strewed this yard; a stone, outdoor fireplace made a squat monument; and the judge had enthroned himself before it. The stranger quietly said, "Good evening." Then: "A patio and a eucalyptus tree. You travel by staying at home, eh, Judge?"

Boaker came ponderously to his feet, extending his hand. "I've wintered in California at times," he said. "They make a fine art of living down there, and this keeps the memory of it green. The eucalyptus took a lot of care, but I'm proud of the accomplishment. Did you ever consider how few men have planted a tree? But you didn't come here to talk about that. It's mighty good to see you again, boy."

The stranger took the proffered hand. "You recognized me when I rode in?"

Boaker shook his silvery head. "Ten years change a boy to a man, but they only make an old man older. But

I've watched every stranger who appeared, knowing you'd come. I wasn't really sure till you made that remark up in my chambers. It was like hearing Cholla Sam Seldon talk."

"I know," the stranger said. "That Texas truism is mighty near Sam's motto. He wired me in Texas. He paid for ten words, and he got 'em. 'When a man needs a gun, he needs it bad.' In two hours I'd turned in my badge, got a leave of absence, and headed north."

He kept his voice low, but it had lost its whispering quality, and even his personality had changed in these brief moments. Some of the grimness was gone, and some of the studied restraint. Boaker said, "You've turned out to be quite a man, Brad. Sam must be proud."

"He cussed me out for being so far away when he needed me," Brad Seldon confessed. "His leg's still in splints from trying to top a rough one in the breaking-corral at S-1. He handed me this job and started me on my way. Said you'd be able to fill in the gaps, Judge."

Boaker sighed. "Sam's getting too old to be ramrodding a syndicate as big as his. Shucks, Seldon ranches are strewed from the Coeur d'Alenes to Fargo. Why haven't you been home managing one, boy, instead of gallivanting all over creation?"

Seldon shrugged. "Sam took me to raise when my folks died, and I'm mighty beholden to him. Since I'm Sam Seldon's nephew, a lot of folks figgered I'd take my pick of his ranches when I come of age. But I didn't aim to lean on him always. A ranger's pay isn't fat, but a man stands on his own feet."

"Stiff-backed Seldon pride!" Boaker snorted with the license of an old and proved friend.

"I'm here to help him now," Seldon said. "What is this big trouble you hinted at in your letters to Sam?"

"To take it from the beginning, the S-5 just about had Hurumpaw Basin to itself at first," Boaker said and waved Seldon to one of the wicker chairs. "Gus Banning always made a good showing for old Sam, as S-5's manager. Then

Ord Wheeler settled here; he was the first of the little fellows; but others came at his heels, men who raise a little stock and break a little sod and between one thing and another manage to keep their heads above water. The Raggedy Pants Pool, they call themselves, now that they've banded against S-5."

"Banning crowded them?"

"Who knows what started it? A cow missing here, a fence cut there. First Banning started building up a crew of hired gunhands; then Wheeler, as leader of the Raggedy Pants boys, brought in Limpy McSwain and four or five friends of Limpy's. That's when I started writing to Cholla Sam. I know Sam always gives his managers plenty of rope, figuring they're doing their chores so long as they maintain the peace and show a profit. But I don't like the looks of the faces you see around Banning's bunkhouse these days."

"Who cracked the first cap?"

"Limpy McSwain, for the Pool," Boaker said emphatically. "Gus Banning had given orders for the little fellows to keep on the east side of Trinity River. Tom Muller and Skeeter Grimes, two of Gus's original crew, came across Limpy and some of his friends on S-5 range. Muller and Grimes weren't packing guns, and when words got to the swearing stage, Limpy shot Muller out of his saddle. Grimes got away with bullets buzzing around him, and it was his testimony that convicted McSwain this morning."

Seldon raised his eyebrows. "But McSwain didn't threaten Grimes in court, did he?"

"No, he called Grimes a fool and laid his tongue on the jury too, saying they were all tools of the S-5 that weren't even smart enough to know they were tools. He became a little more personal when he got around to me and the sheriff and Gary Strawn. Limpy claimed that S-5 owned the law in Hurumpaw and that he was being railroaded, not for murder, but for bucking the big ranch. He threatened Gus Banning, too. Said he'd live to see Gus hang, along with the rest of us. I'm admitting it gave me a turn, Brad, and I think it scared Gary Strawn, too. That's why Strawn was so touchy when you insinuated he was afraid. There's more poison in Limpy McSwain's soul than you'll find in a barrel of rattlesnakes."

Seldon frowned thoughtfully. "I saw Cholla Sam's map of S-5 back at the headquarters ranch," he said. "Trinity River cuts diagonally across the basin, running from the northwest to the southeast. As I understand it, the southwest part of the basin is all Seldon land, the range stretching south almost to this town. Is that the straight of it?"

"Now you're putting your finger on the trouble," Boaker said. "Trinity River's always been the accepted boundary, yes. And whoever controls the Trinity controls Hurumpaw Basin. That makes it even-steven; Seldon holdings and Raggedy Pants holdings both border on the river, which means that both have riparian rights. But S-5's range was pre-empted land at first, Cholla Sam getting legal claim after the homesteading laws were passed, so the old border was a pretty nebulous affair. A lot of those old-time surveys were made from a hotel window, anyway. Maybe the Trinity's the true boundary; maybe it's not."

"And if it isn't?"

Boaker shook his head. "Then the lid blows off. If the Trinity actually runs on Raggedy Pants land only, Cholla Sam might as well sell his acreage for ten cents on the dollar and uncork a bottle of red ink as far as S-5 is concerned. On the other hand, if the Trinity belongs solely to the Seldon Syndicate, the Raggedy Pants Pool is going to have to ride to war or fold up. And with Gus Banning keeping a chip on his shoulder, it's likely too late to settle this thing peacefully."

"Then," said Seldon with a certain satisfaction, "my work is cut out for me."

"Meaning—?"

"Meaning I've got to stop a range war. I know Cholla Sam's feelings on such matters, and *I'm* Cholla Sam as far as this deal is concerned. Sam never dodged a good fight, but he didn't believe in building dollars on blood, either. If the word goes out that a Seldon ranch is crowding its neighbors, then we'll find suspicion against us on every range from Idaho to Dakota where Seldon cattle graze. A man's lifetime reputation is at stake, and I'm the one who's got to stand up for him. And the first thing is to settle this boundary business once and forever. Then we'll know who's in the right."

Boaker said, "I've taken care of that. Since I sent my last letter to Cholla Sam. Get me right, Brad; I'm Sam's friend. But I'm also part of the law of Hurumpaw, and I'm out for fair play no matter how the cards fall. I had Gary Strawn send for Charlie Fenton, a good, capable man who takes surveying contracts from the government. Fenton's on his way now to give Hurumpaw Basin a real going over."

"That suits me," said Seldon and came to a stand. "There's one more question I've got to ask, Judge. Does anybody besides you know that Cholla Sam Seldon intended sending me down here to represent him?"

"Nary a soul," Boaker said. "And what about your side of it, boy? Why this impersonation of Hush Considine?"

"I remembered your letters to Sam," Seldon said. "You mentioned that Gus Banning was hiring gun-toting hardcases for the S-5. Maybe Banning himself needs to be looking for another job; maybe he's doing what he thinks is best for Cholla Sam Seldon. I've got to find out which, before I pass judgment. As long as he's hiring gunhands, I thought he might like to hire Hush Considine. Hush is an easy man to impersonate, with his foofaraw garb and his queer voice." He smiled thinly. "Besides," he added, "on a job like this, it might help to be a gent not given to talking."

Boaker grinned. "There's another Texas truism: 'Keep silent in the saddle and you'll stick your horse the longest.'

Good idea, boy. But we know of Hush Considine up this way, and, by the same token, horseback news could carry some queer stories south of Texas. Supposing Hush Considine heard them?"

"He won't," said Seldon. "He's dead. I know; it was my Ranger company that got him. And because the boys wanted to get a line on certain friends of Considine's, they didn't do any shouting about what had happened to Hush. I wired my captain from S-1, asking him to continue keeping the news quiet until I gave him the sign."

Some disconcerting thought put a crease in Boaker's forehead, and he said, "Limpy McSwain hangs tomorrow, Brad. Maybe that will mean the lid blows off. Ord Wheeler's kept inside the law so far; but Limpy McSwain drew Raggedy Pants pay, which means that Wheeler may put up a fight for him. Especially since Limpy's friends will likely prod Wheeler. How does all that fit into your scheme of things, boy?"

Seldon's mouth tightened into a straight and unrelenting line, and he said, "I've been a Texas Ranger these past five years, Judge. It's been my business to run down men of McSwain's breed and give them their needings. McSwain's killing of Tom Muller was out-and-out murder, and if it means starting the very range war I'm trying to stop, I'll still be for hanging him. I reckon Cholla Sam Seldon would see it the same way."

"Yes, I reckon he would," Boaker agreed. "Now do you know everything you need to know?"

Seldon remembered the girl who wanted Limpy McSwain to live, and he remembered the offer she had made and the mystery that went with it, but he had given a promise to her and he said, "Everything. And thank you, Judge. I don't know whether Cholla Sam has you written down in his ledgers, but you're one of his biggest assets."

He put his hand out to the eucalyptus and he said, "You're like this tree, Judge—sturdy and dependable and grown straight through all the years. I may come to you again. But I'll ask no favor that any other man, Ord Wheeler, for instance, couldn't ask you. And now I'll be getting along to see about earning that fifty dollars that was promised me."

Gravely he gave his hand to this old man, and then he strode out of the yard, his somber garb blending with the night and his silver spurs making muted music as he headed back toward town.

3 : Little Miss Mystery

At this evening hour Calumet should have been aboil with the beginnings of its varied and blatant night life, the dust stirring to the milling hoofs of incoming cowhorses, the bars and the gaming tables claiming the far-flung citizenry of Hurumpaw's range. A hundred such towns as this Calumet had familiarized Brad Seldon with this unchanging pattern; frame or adobe, Montana or Texas, it was always the same. But he came along the boardwalks of a grave and silent town that was held tight by an inward tension needing no translating.

In passing, he had his brief glimpse over the batwings of some of the saloons, finding a solemn hush as townsmen stood quietly at the bars or made listless talk at the tables. The hitchrails, so crowded before the law's edict had sent the Raggedy Pants Pool out of town, were still empty; the bevy of buckboards was gone from before the courthouse, the brick structure standing dark and mute. There was light, though, in the long log and frame building that flanked the courthouse to the south. Barred windows laid a striped, saffron pattern upon the ground, and the high silhouette of the gallows beside the jail stood gaunt against the first starlight.

Seldon came into the jail and past its cubbyhole of an office and down the shadowy corridor of the cell block, a dim and dismal tunnel in the uncertain light of overhanging kerosene lamps. A short, powerfully built man lolled upon a hard bench, and Seldon recognized him as the deputy who had laboriously climbed to the roof of a store that afternoon to line his sights on the veranda of the Silverbow.

Unabashed, the deputy said, "Evening. I'm Buck Prentiss. Lookin' for somebody, Considine?"

"Endicott around?"

"Sheriff's getting a late supper. Him and Gary Strawn went over to the Elite."

Seldon took out the makings, fashioned himself a cigarette, and passed tobacco and papers over to Prentiss. The smoke going, Seldon said, "How's the prisoner?"

Prentiss jerked a thumb. "Take a look," he invited. "But don't get close enough to let him bite you. Not if you don't want hydrophobia."

Seldon stepped toward the indicated cell, and there was light enough to see the high-shouldered form of the man who paced its narrow width. No flash and foofaraw gunman, this Limpy McSwain wore a faded blue denim shirt and Levis that were glazed with dirt and colorless from long use. His face was square and arrogant, his jaw and cheeks and upper lip shadowed by the blue-black of a week's stubble. He dragged his left leg in a peculiar, shuffling limp, and his eyes were hot and yellow, the hell in them kept at a perpetual boil. His was a feline savagery, stark and primal, the rending, slashing savagery of claw and fang.

Looking at McSwain, Seldon could see Tom Muller, unarmed and helpless, going down before the hate of this man, and could understand how it had been. Wonderingly, he said aloud, "A thousand cold, round dollars—!"

McSwain curled his lip and loosed blasphemy until his breath was spent, and Seldon turned silently away. Buck Prentiss said, "A sweet customer, eh? And I have to listen to him all night." His tone was bantering, but there was a rind of sweat on his upper lip, and his eyes were afraid.

Seldon said, "Think his friends will show up?"

Prentiss shrugged.

"They'll have to cross the river if they do," Seldon mused. "Which bridge would they likely use?"

"Raggedy Pants men have to ride out of their way to cross the railroad bridge east of town," Prentiss explained. "There's another bridge, away up in the northwest corner of the basin. That ain't so handy either. Ord Wheeler will use Cowper's Ford."

"Far from here?"

"Not as the crow flies," Prentiss said and went on to talk of trails and directions and landmarks, drawing with a stubby forefinger an invisible map on the bench's pants-polished surface. When he'd finished, Seldon said, "Tell Endicott I've taken a pasear. I'll be back by morning."

Leaving the jail, he crossed to the livery stable, found the same hostler who'd served him earlier, paid the man, and did his own saddling. Astride the roan, he stirred the street's dust, walking the mount until the last dwelling had fallen behind, then lifting the gelding to a high gallop, keeping his eye on a rough, saw-toothed notch in the tumbled outlines of the Hurumpaw Hills along the eastern horizon. The unreeling miles brought him into rougher country, a land broken by coulees and the upthrust of bluffs; and he crossed this tangled terrain and dipped down into the breaks of the Trinity and came to the river's western bank.

He dismounted here, shadowed by the crowding willows, and he listened to the brawling voice of the waters and saw the starlight dance on the stream's yellow crest, drinking in the beauty of the scene and drawing out the moment to a long fullness. Then, his mind upon the things Buck Prentiss had told him, he judged that he was above the ford, so he searched out a trail among the willows and paralleled the river in its southeasterly flow.

Cowper's Ford was only a mile below, and he knew when he neared it by the difference in the river's voice; the water that rushed so boisterously above seeming to idle here, as though tired from its rough and rocky travels out of the upper basin. A dugway leading down to the stream bore the markings of many hoofs, and he studied these by matchlight and found the sign to his liking. Many riders had come and gone this way, but none of them within the last two or three hours.

Satisfied, he headed up the trail away from the river, unsaddled the roan and hobbled it and turned the mount loose to graze. In the shadow of a rocky buttress which pointed a mossy thumb at the sky, he spread the saddle blanket, put the kak into position as a pillow, stripped off his boots and gun-belt, and in five minutes he was fast asleep.

Long riding and the strains of a varied day had taken toll of him, yet if part of his mind lay smothered by deep and dreamless sleep, part of it also stood sentinel, alert to each alien sound of the night. Five years with the Texas Rangers had made that trait an ingrained part of him; he had learned wariness because it often meant the measure of a man's life span. Thus the first splash of hoofs in the nearby stream brought him awake, but for a moment he lay unmoving, his eyes open. Then he was pulling on his boots.

The new day was here, murky and gray and made misty by the river's nearness, the chill of the night still lingering and the sun not yet showing itself over the ramparts of the Hurumpaws. Gauging the time that was left to him, he made quick and useful movements, rolling up the blanket, latching on his gun-belt. He had a look at the Colt's loads, too; but when the first horseman breasted the rise up from the ford, Brad Seldon was sitting with his back to the rocky buttress, putting a match to a new-spun cigarette.

"Howdy," Seldon said in that studied whisper of his, and Ord Wheeler reined up abruptly, surprise raising his dark and heavy brows.

Wheeler said, "You'd be that new special deputy—the gunhawk who drifted into town yesterday. What in blazes are you doing here?"

"I've come," said Seldon, "to see that you don't ride

on into town to make a nuisance of yourself by trying to stop Limpy McSwain from being hung."

There were all of twenty-five riders to back Ord Wheeler; they came heaving into view, dim and indistinct in this first light, men of varying ages and temperaments welded into one by the singleness of their purpose. They were of a type that Seldon knew, men who filed on a parcel of land, gambling their strength and their years against all the circumstances that might conspire to keep them from making a poor man's living. But there were others in this group too, and he could tell them as easily as he could have distinguished wolves from sheep dogs; and gauging the hard and predatory look of the few, Seldon knew them to be the men Limpy McSwain had fetched along when he'd come to draw Raggedy Pants pay.

It was one of these who eyed Seldon and said, "He must 'a' heard so many yarns about his own rep that he got to believin' 'em!"

But Wheeler, his blunt jaw tight with suspicion, said, "You're here alone? To stop *us?*"

"Count me again," Seldon suggested. "I'm only one."

Wheeler took on the look of a man torn between anger and derision. "How in thunder," he demanded, "do you figger on doing the trick?"

Seldon shrugged. "I gave that a lot of thought," he confessed. "I could have hunkered on top of this rock and tossed a little lead. That might have slowed you down long enough for the law to take care of Limpy. But you'd have rooted me out and a few good men would have got killed —including me. I don't figger Limpy's worth that. So I decided to make it a man-to-man proposition."

Wheeler sucked in his breath. "Meaning—?"

"Me and you," Seldon said. "We fight it out. If I beat you, then you get yourself and these boys back across the Trinity. Beat me, and you've opened the trail to Calumet."

"I'll be damned!" Wheeler said, almost reverently.

But one of those who looked like he might have ridden with McSwain plucked at the big man's sleeve and said, "The trail's already open. You don't have to do this, Ord. He's running a bluff, and he's a dead man right now, if we want it that way."

Wheeler shook off the other's fingers. "No, I don't have to do business your way," he said to Seldon. "I spent my years learning to handle a rope and a branding iron while you were making a fine art out of killing. I'm not ashamed of being out of your class as a gunman."

"How are you fixed for fists?" Seldon asked. "Or do you want to crawl out of that, too?"

He brought the high flush of anger to Wheeler's face, and Wheeler stepped down out of his saddle, fumbling at his gun-belt and saying, "I'm buying a hunk of your proposition, mister! Maybe I'm crazy, for I could see you dead instead; but I'd keep remembering that you died thinking I was afraid of you."

Some of the tension left Seldon then. He had based this gamble upon the quick estimate he had made of Ord Wheeler in that single glimpse of the man in Calumet, plus the things Judge Boaker had said about Wheeler. And having played a risky game with only a reckless faith in his chances, Seldon had thus suddenly won.

Voices rose in a confused babble at Wheeler's back. Someone said, "Clear the trail, Ord, and let's get riding. You'll find your fighting here; the rest of us will get a share in Calumet. Hurry, boy; we're keeping the S-5 waiting."

Seldon stiffened. *"The S-5 is in town?"* he asked incredulously.

"They were headed that way at midnight," Wheeler snapped. "Do you think we've been asleep? Just because we let Easy Endicott run us out of town doesn't mean that we haven't been keeping a finger on things. And if Banning's crew can attend a hanging, so can we!"

Then he came charging at Seldon with a wild flurry of fists, and this wasn't the time for reflection upon the powder-keg potentialities that would come in Calumet if the two factions met. Seldon had to put all his faculties on the fight; and he did, sidestepping Wheeler's first rush and swinging the man around with a hard blow to the shoulder.

Out of a saddle, Wheeler loomed much bigger. He stood no taller than Seldon; but he bulked broader, a huge and hard-muscled man, wide-shouldered and with the narrow hips that a saddle hews. Seldon barely rocked the man with that first blow, and he followed it with a devil's tattoo upon Wheeler's face and body, feinting for openings and bewildering the homesteader with the swiftness of the attack.

But Wheeler took his pound of flesh in payment for Seldon's razzle-dazzle audacity. Wheeler didn't have the knack of planting a blow with precision, but wild swinging netted him some results. His fists were rocky, one catching Seldon along the neck to send him spinning; and Seldon went down to his knees. Voices roared, beseeching Wheeler to press this advantage; but Seldon was back on his feet before Wheeler got himself going again. His head whirling, Seldon closed with the man, clinging tightly until the earth ceased its rocking, then breaking free to dance backward as Wheeler's knuckles glanced off the hard flesh armoring Seldon's ribs.

Men had come down out of saddles and formed into a close-packed ring, uproarious with advice and encouragement for Wheeler. But Seldon's blows had taken toll, and Wheeler's movements were erratic; yet the Pool leader plunged forward with grim and determined intent. Seldon almost tripped over a deadfall log in his retreat, and he pivoted quickly, clipping Wheeler's blunt chin at the same time. Wheeler went to his knees, but Seldon had lost his balance, and he caromed against the men who ringed him.

That was when he caught a quick and nebulous movement with the corner of his eye, and he made a desperate effort to move away. He had come up hard against the man who had urged Wheeler not to fight; and just as he realized that the fellow was swinging a gun barrel at him, he felt the blow and his knees unhinged beneath him; and he went down, fighting against the roaring, swirling darkness.

Wheeler was calling a man's name and cursing that name, and Seldon had that one last glimpse of the Pool leader, reading the anger and dismay in Wheeler's face and trying to hold on to the sight of it as a last bridge between reality and oblivion. And then the lights went out for Seldon.

He had no means of measuring the time he swam through interminable darkness, fighting back toward consciousness; when he opened his eyes, the sky looked no lighter than it had before, and he judged that he had been out only a matter of minutes. But in that brief span, the Raggedy Pants Pool had ridden on, leaving Brad Seldon quite alone. Except for the girl.

She sat on that same deadfall log that had almost tripped him, and he could have opened his eyes to a worse sight; for her face, glimpsed so briefly in Calumet last night, stood the test of the dawn. A six-shooter dangled in her right hand.

"So it's little Miss Mystery," he said and grinned weakly. Then he came erect, taking his own slow time at it and reeling with the first steps. Instantly the gun leveled in her hand. He glimpsed a saddled horse tied to a nearby bush, and he said, "I don't remember your being in the crowd."

"I wasn't," she said. "I came riding up just as you got clouted with a gun barrel. Ord didn't like that kind of finish for his fight, but it opened the trail to Calumet just the same. He asked me to keep you here for a few hours, just to make sure the trail stays open."

"So you're still out to save Limpy McSwain's neck," he said.

Her voice turned tired and hopeless. "McSwain never meant anything to me one way or the other. The thing I was fighting for is probably lost. But I'm not here to palaver with you."

Groaning, he pressed his hand to his head and took another step toward her. The ground had grown steady for him, but there was no proof of it in the way he lurched. A yard from the log's end, he said, *"Watch out!"* And at the same time he kicked hard against the log's rounded surface.

She went spilling over backward, and he was instantly plunging toward her. In a swift blur of motion he got the gun twisted out of her hand with no great harm to her; and he pulled her erect then, holding her at arm's length and making his say before her startled anger gave her voice.

"Sorry. There's too much at stake to play ladies and gentlemen today," he explained. "My horse is grazing somewhere nearby; you'll find him hobbled, and my saddle's by the rock. Help yourself, if you're so minded. I'm taking your cayuse to save me minutes. If you want to swap back, I'll be in Calumet."

He spied his own gun-belt beside the log, and he picked it up and latched it around his middle and tossed her gun toward the bushes. All this she watched in silence, then she said evenly, "It's too bad Ord didn't let them kill you!"

But he was already running toward her horse, and he made it into the saddle without touching the stirrups. Leaning to pluck at the tie-rope, he saw the brand then, big and bold on the mount's left shoulder and out of his sight until now. That brand was an S-5; and because by that token the girl belonged to S-5 and was therefore a traitor to the brand, his astonishment was vast. But there wasn't time for the dozen clamoring questions he might have put to her—not when he knew this urgent need to get to Calumet before Hurumpaw's range started its war.

4 : Hangtown

Hard riding fetched Brad Seldon across the miles to Calumet in record time, for fear and desperation were quirt and spur, and this borrowed S-5 saddler was built for speed. Seldon put the river breaks behind him, blowing his horse on the last high rise, and the minutes that he lost in the tangled land of buttes and coulees beyond were regained on the flat desolation that stretched southward to where the town's smoke curled.

He came expecting to find guns and death, and to witness a range's ruin in the making. He came with the deep and bitter knowledge that all he had hoped to gain in Hurumpaw Basin might already be forever lost. He rode with a worried man's oblivion to the bruises Ord Wheeler's fists had given him. And he found Calumet held by a tight and deceptive calm when he reached the main street's eastern end. The storm had yet to break.

But the thunderheads were gathered, for Ord Wheeler had brought his full force here; Raggedy Pants saddlers stood at every hitchrail, and the men from across the Trinity were scattered along the boardwalks and beneath the wooden awnings of sundry establishments, all of them making a great show of indolent lounging, all of them tense with a sullen, resigned expectancy.

They gave Seldon varied glances as he rode along the street's bleakness, some of them blinking in surprise, some staring woodenly, but no man made a challenging motion. There was this sign that the Pool still respected the law that he temporarily represented, and Seldon wondered if they would hold to that respect until the real showdown came.

Ord Wheeler, himself, made a big, blocky figure on the Silverbow's veranda; he looked at Seldon and at Seldon's borrowed mount, and then he smiled, but there was no mirth in him. Wheeler lifted his hand in a gesture that might have meant anything, and Seldon returned that half-salute with still-faced gravity and went on his way toward the courthouse.

The yard before that rusty building, littered yesterday by Raggedy Pants saddlers and wagons, now held the anchored horses of the S-5, a good score of them, their riders huddled together and waiting silently. Seldon, giving the scene his inspection, saw a quick and ready parallel; here was the powder keg, and strewed along the street was a fuse made out of quick-tempered men, and yonder, standing stark against the day's first light, was the gallows—a match to set off the explosion. Voices hummed steadily from the jail building; and Seldon stepped down from his saddle, left his horse among the others, and made his way to the log and frame structure.

The cubbyhole office to the building's front was crammed with men; the law of Hurumpaw was here in the heavy form of Easy Endicott and his two deputies, Buck Prentiss and Sid Greenleaf. Gary Strawn lounged in a corner, and Judge Boaker paced restlessly wherever there was room to permit his passage. Two other men, strangers to Seldon, were backed against the wall. Endicott favored Seldon with a dark frown and said, "So here you are! I'd 'a' laid a bet you'd lit out for Texas."

Buck Prentiss said, "I told you he asked the way to Cowper's Ford, Easy. Look at the marks on his face. I'm beginning to get me a hunch how Ord Wheeler came by the black eye he's got."

"Okay, okay," Endicott snapped with the sudden irritation of a man weighted by responsibility. "I'll grant he's been on the job—in his own way. He's here now, and that's what counts. We'll need every gun we've got."

One of the strangers, a big man garbed in riding breeches, said, "Who is this fellow, Easy?"

"Considine, Gus," Endicott said. "Hush Considine, the Texas gunhawk. He's a special deputy until this dirty job is over. Considine, meet Gus Banning of the S-5, and Poe Munger, his foreman."

"Pleased," Seldon whispered and took his look at the pair. Banning, he observed, was one of those men who wear their years gracefully, and there were forty and more behind him. Clean-shaven and with a trace of talcum on his cheeks, he'd have been handsome except for a certain flabbiness of features and a network of wrinkles around his eyes and mouth. Munger looked much more the range man. Lath-lean, the segundo was stooped from long dodging of low doorways, and his eyes were narrowed to the perpetual squint of one who scans sun-drenched prairies. He looked like a man given to laziness and easy living, but that was only at first glance. There was something hard about his mouth, and his smile reminded Seldon of a wolf's way of baring its teeth.

Judge Boaker suddenly said, "I see no use in waiting. McSwain was to be hanged this morning, but no hour was mentioned. Well, it's morning. Those Pool boys are going to stay in town until something happens. If there has to be a showdown when we use the gallows, we might as well have it now."

"That's right as rain," Gus Banning said. "Take McSwain out and give him his needings, Easy. And if it's guns you want, you can swear in every one of my S-5 hands as temporary deputies. That's why I fetched 'em."

"And wave a red flag at a bull?" Endicott snapped. "We've been over this before, Gus. What do you think the Raggedy Pants boys will do if they find S-5 helping to hang their man?"

"I don't give a damn!" Banning exploded and temper

reddened his cheeks. "Tom Muller was one of my men. He died with a bullet in his back. I'm staying here till I see Limpy McSwain hung!"

Judge Boaker said, "You didn't go out of your way for Tom when he was alive, Gus. Aren't you a little late taking up for him?"

"Now listen—!" Poe Munger began in a flat, truculent voice, and Seldon took a sideward step toward the man, seeing here the makings of a lesser explosion that could reverberate to the street's end. But Endicott, pressed beyond all patience, said, "That'll be enough! I could order you out of town, Banning, but I guess you've got a right to witness the hanging. But so has Wheeler and his outfit. And now you'd better get back to your boys. But remember this: Any man without a badge who cracks a cap makes himself an outlaw. And I don't care what brand he rides for!"

"There'll be another election one of these days," Banning said darkly and thrust his way out of the office, Munger silently following him. Gary Strawn broke his own long silence to say, "Now we've got *them* against us, too."

"If you want it official, Easy," Boaker put in, "I'm giving you your orders. McSwain hangs at once. Have you got an extra gun I could borrow?"

Endicott fumbled in a desk and produced a forty-five which he passed to the judge. Greenleaf and Prentiss, stationed near the door, shifted restlessly, and the sheriff said, "You heard the judge, boys. You two fetch Limpy along. Make it fast, but make it right. Give him a minute to speak his piece, and listen to any reasonable request he makes. But I want that gallows sprung before all hell lets loose. The rest of us will see that you're left alone to do your work."

Strawn shifted his holster an inch forward, gnawing nervously at his mustache. Boaker looked to the loads of his borrowed gun, and only Seldon remained unmoving. Down the jail's narrow corridor, as dim now as it had been by lamplight, a key grated and the foul mouthings of Mc-Swain filled the air. They brought the limping man out with his hands bound behind him, and the two deputies came steering him up the corridor. Easy Endicott said, "All set? Here we go, boys!"

The sheriff and Seldon came out of the building first, shoulder to shoulder and moving neither swiftly nor slowly. Strawn and Boaker were at their heels, and the two deputies with their cursing prisoner came pacing behind. Over Calumet the hush still held, the S-5 men standing grouped before the courthouse, the Raggedy Pants riders strung out along the street. The sun had reared itself above the Hurumpaw's eastern ramparts and stood poised on a lofty peak, stretching its arms and smiling. It was, Seldon reflected, no day for dying. He drew the fresh cleanness of the morning deep into his lungs, and Ord Wheeler moved from the Silverbow's porch, his raised voice carrying clear in the silence.

"Endicott!" Wheeler called. "We're giving you thirty seconds to turn McSwain loose."

The sheriff said nothing, his lips grown tighter and all the geniality gone out of him. The seven rounded the building and came to the foot of the gallows, and by this time every Raggedy Pants man was gone from Calumet's street. Like tumbleweeds scattered by a rising wind, they'd scurried to the shadowy slots between buildings, and Seldon read this sign and recognized its portent and wondered when the fury would break.

This gallows that reared above them had served Hurumpaw County across the years, and it stood grim and sturdy and waiting. At the steps leading up to its high platform with the cross-arm and the dangling noose, McSwain said, "Hurry it up, and be damned! I've only got one wish to make, and that's to see all of you choking out your lives at the end of a rope. And I'll do it yet!"

His hot and yellowish eyes touched each of them

briefly, lighting at last on Seldon. "You too, stranger!" Mc-Swain said, his savagery almost tangible.

"Up the steps, McSwain!" squat Buck Prentiss ordered, the fear still in his eyes. And that was when the guns began their barking.

Those sixes were speaking from a dozen different points where Raggedy Pants men had posted themselves, but the first hail of lead fell short of any solid target, kicking up the dust in warning. Instantly Boaker and Strawn and Seldon and the sheriff fanned out, seeking whatever cover they could find in the gallows lot. Over across the street, between the livery stable and the blacksmith shop next to it, Seldon spied a barrel with the word *Fire* painted on it in red letters that had run to long, dripping legs, and he made it to that flimsy protection in an oblique, zigzagging run. Sheltered, he knelt with gun in hand to trigger at the smoke puffs up the street.

Endicott and the others were returning the fire too, Judge Boaker making an incongruous figure with his silvery hair tousled and a gun in his fist, Strawn stretched behind a heap of debris and firing with cool and deliberate calculation. Only Greenleaf and Prentiss had kept their guns cased. The two deputies were urging McSwain up the steps, and with the three of them on the high platform, they made large and easy targets. But Limpy McSwain stood between the deputies and the questing guns; so long as the platform was under him, he was their protection from Raggedy Pants lead.

The street was echoing now to the steady beat of gunfire, and the S-5 saddlers before the courthouse reared and pitched and squealed, some breaking free of the hitchrails. S-5's crew had placed itself behind the horses, the men milling excitedly, and Endicott's voice rose stridently. *"Banning!"* the sheriff shouted. *"Stay out of this, damn you!"*

Here was the moment when anything might have happened, and a quick charge of Raggedy Pants men would mean that sheer numbers would sweep them to the gallows and the saving of Limpy McSwain. Reloading his gun, Seldon sent a hasty glance at Prentiss and Greenleaf, seeing them adjust the noose over McSwain's head, taking an endless moment to do that simple chore.

Someone up the street had marked Seldon's cover; a bullet droned out of nothingness to smash in a barrel stave and water came spurting upon him. He fired three shots so quickly that the sound blurred together. He thought, *God, don't let Banning lose his head!* And then, even above the roar of the gunfire, he was certain he heard the twang of the hangrope.

When he had his look, the rope stretched taut, and Limpy McSwain was gone from view, down through the trapdoor, and Prentiss and Greenleaf, no longer protected by McSwain's presence, had flattened themselves out on the platform. Lead sleeted against the gallows, a heavy, angry barrage, and then, suddenly, the guns went silent, a great sigh going up from many men and the town itself seeming to shudder. And in the midst of this lull Sheriff Easy Endicott reared to his feet and came waddling out into the street.

"Wheeler!" he called. "Show yourself. I want to make talk."

Ord Wheeler came around the Elite Café with all the caution of a man who has learned to trust nobody. Endicott asked, "Any of your men hurt?"

"As far as I know, only one," Wheeler said gruffly. "A nick in the leg. Why, lawman?"

"I see blood on Sid Greenleaf's sleeve," Endicott said. "But from the way Sid's carrying himself, it can't be any real hurt. That makes it even—a scratch for a scratch. Limpy's dead, Wheeler. Nothing you can do now can bring him back to life. What do you say we call it off?"

Wheeler made no instant answer, his dark brow corrugated with thought, and Endicott added, "I could outlaw the bunch of you for this, if I was so minded. And I'll have to, if this ain't the end of it. But Limpy McSwain was your man, and I know you figgered like him—that S-5's power hung him. That's why I'm not holding it against you for the play you made. So take your choice. Do you aim to finish out a dead man's hand?"

This Endicott had soared in Seldon's estimation when he'd ordered Gus Banning out of his office earlier, and he rose even higher now as he made this stand, trading tolerance for peace and showing a wise man's understanding. But there were still the makings of big trouble. Boaker and Strawn had come into the street, taking a stand behind Endicott, and Raggedy Pants men were drifting from cover. But S-5's crew was moving up from the courthouse, Banning and Munger in the lead, and Ord Wheeler had not yet spoken.

Banning said, "I heard your proposition, Sheriff. Do you mean to say these fellows can ride out of here free and easy after shooting up the town and trying to buck the law?"

"Gus," Endicott said without turning to face the man, "do you *want* a range war?"

Banning's face took on that high, red flush, and his anger choked him. But Ord Wheeler spoke then. "Maybe you're right, Sheriff," Wheeler said. "There's one thing that can't be changed. McSwain's dead, and all the powder-burning in the world won't make him alive. I—!"

His words dwindled, a look of shocked incredulity coming over his face as he suddenly spun half around, his hand going to his shoulder spasmodically as a gun laid its flat crash against the new silence. Wheeler had been shot! And in the very instant that Seldon grasped that fact, Raggedy Pants men and S-5's crew were stridently cursing and reaching for guns. And with the peace that Easy Endicott had preserved now tottering on a thin and crumbling edge, Seldon saw his man and made his play.

The glint of sunlight on a gun barrel gave him his cue, drawing his eye to the roof of the jail building. He could only glimpse a man's head and one shoulder, but that made target enough, and his gun was still in his hand. He brought up the Colt and triggered once; and a man reared himself to a high erectness, teetered for a breathless instant, and then came somersaulting downward, turning over in midair and lighting hard on the boardwalk before the jail.

"Have a look at him!" Seldon cried, not whispering now. *"Have a look before you start the fireworks!"*

That turned the tide. All factions went on a run toward the sprawled figure, Raggedy Pants men jostling S-5 hands, and the law caught in the middle, and they turned over this bushwhacker and had their look at him, and Seldon recognized him instantly. He didn't know the fellow's name, and he was never to know it, but he was that same lean and predatory man who'd ridden into Calumet with Ord Wheeler this morning—the one who'd urged Wheeler not to make a fair fight at Cowper's Ford, and who'd swung a gun barrel at Seldon's head to end that fight.

"God!" Endicott breathed. "Now why was *he* turning a gun against Wheeler?"

There was nobody to give him answer, and the crisis was gone. Somebody was cutting away Wheeler's coat, and the wound that was bared was nothing to give a man great worry. Flanked by his friends, the Raggedy Pants leader headed up the street to where a doctor's shingle swayed, and the S-5 hands went silently and sullenly to their mounts. Boaker and Strawn moved toward the courthouse, while Seldon, suddenly aware that his work as a lawman was finished, crossed to the horse he'd ridden. Endicott waddled after him, and when the sheriff got a look at the mount, he said, "Fay Abbott's sorrel! How do you come by this cayuse?"

"Oh, the girl?" Seldon said. "I met her on the trail. I needed a fresh horse, and she agreed to swap. Who is she?"

"Bookkeeper out at S-5," Endicott said. "I wonder if Gus will appreciate her doing you a favor."

Seldon shrugged. "I'll have to return the cayuse. How do I find S-5's headquarters? I could tag after that crew that's riding out, but I think Banning will need time to cool before he sees another lawman again. Even an ex-lawman."

"Straight north is the way the crow would fly it," Endicott said. "But a stranger would maybe find it easier to head over to the Trinity and follow it upstream. You'll come to a place where you'll be able to see the ranch buildings from the bank." He paused, a new thought taking hold of him. "You've got fifty dollars coming," he added. "Step over to my office and I'll pay you."

Across the way, Buck Prentiss was laboring along toward the gallows with an empty coffin on his broad back. Seldon watched the deputy put down the box and open a door beneath the gallows platform and disappear from sight. Jerking his thumb toward the sprawled figure that still lay before the jail building, Seldon said, "Use the money to buy him a box and a hole in the ground. The county will bury Limpy, but no man's going to be fool enough to claim that other body."

"I see what you mean," Endicott said and frowned. "Whoever paid that long-geared galoot to be handy to take a shot at Wheeler is a man who wanted to see hell let loose on this range. And that little scheme would have worked if you hadn't moved so fast. The Raggedy Pants boys thought S-5 lead had got Wheeler for sure. Until they had their look."

"That's how I figured it," Seldon admitted and led his horse toward the Silverbow. There was time now for the breakfast he hadn't eaten, and as he walked along he smiled to himself with the thought that a thick beefsteak, nestled against his backbone, might have made a quick and telling difference in that fight he'd had with Ord Wheeler at Cowper's Ford.

5 : **River Rendezvous**

Fay Abbott of the S-5, seeing the man she knew as Hush
Considine ride off toward Calumet on her own sorrel saddler, made a quick run for the pistol he'd taken from her
and tossed into the bushes. But once the gun was in her
hand, she held it indecisively; the black-garbed rider, top-
ping a rise, vanished from sight, and her moment was lost.
Striding over to Seldon's saddle, beneath the rocky buttress, she gave the kak a hard and angry kick, thereby
bruising her toe. She did a one-legged dance then, holding
her hurt toe in her hands, and when it was over she sat
upon that deadfall log again and began laughing at the
sorry spectacle she must have made.

Seldon's own horse was somewhere yonder, and she
could have caught up the mount and given chase. But Seldon's trail led to Calumet, and Ord Wheeler had exacted
this girl's solemn promise that she'd keep out of the town
this dangerous day. Now she faced the prospect of a long
and lonely vigil, and the laughter ran out of her with the
thought of the tragedy that might be when men came riding back from Calumet. She didn't want to dwell on that,
so she went in search of Seldon's mount to give herself
something to do.

Finding the hobbled animal not far away, she spent
many minutes wooing the roan, and she got the blanket
and saddle and bridle onto the horse with no great trouble,
but she climbed into the kak gingerly. It would be just like
that black-garbed gunhawk, she decided, to leave her a
horse that would set her on her head in a sage clump. But

after taking the early morning kinks out of himself, the roan settled to a tractable trot as Fay headed up river.

She rode with no real point or purpose, letting the roan set its own erratic pace, but keeping close to the Trinity. To the north and west the land veered upward, and she came at last to a high and windswept promontory where she could sit her saddle and have a sweeping view to all the hill-hemmed horizons. With the sun climbing and the air clear, she could even see across the tangled land of buttes and coulees to the shimmering rooftops of Calumet, the town looking deceptively near in the thin air of this high country. To her left ran the river, and at this point the channel was obstructed and the swift pace of the current broken by a sandy, brush-covered island not more than a hundred yards long and fashioned to the shape of a tear-drop.

She knew this island well, for she had visited it many times; a rider could walk a horse from either bank without wetting a boot, the crossing providing a ford as good as Cowper's, except that it was too far upstream to serve the Raggedy Pants men who were strung half the basin's length on the Trinity's eastern bank. That island was neutral ground, if any existed in the basin, but the island didn't interest her at the moment; she kept her eyes to the south, and, before much time had elapsed, she saw a dust cloud wrought by a group of horsemen who came riding out of Calumet. They were headed almost due north, and by that token she knew them to be S-5's crew.

That interested her greatly, for it took two factions to make a war, and here was one leaving the town, apparently in full force. Some time thereafter a lone rider also stirred the dust, but the distance was far too great for recognition, and she lost sight of him when he dipped into that tangled terrain between Calumet and the Trinity. The sun was swinging higher; she became aware that she was hungry, but she knew a greater need than the one for food, so she lingered still; and at long last another dust cloud raised

itself on the flat desolation to the south. This latest cavalcade was aimed for Cowper's Ford, and she drew in her
breath in a quick, sobbing sigh, for this must be the Raggedy Pants Pool riding home again.

She wished she could count heads, but that was impossible, yet there was heart-warming satisfaction in the
sign that as many men had ridden out of Calumet as had
ridden into the town. Wives and children waited on the
Trinity's east bank, and she'd shared their waiting and their
fears this morning, even though she'd kept her vigil alone.
And when the sun stood at zenith, and she'd made a careful reckoning of Ord Wheeler's progress, she urged the
roan down the promontory and through the fringing willows and into the river, hoisting her boots to the saddle
horn's level and riding dry shod to the little island.

Leading the horse back through the tangled thicket,
she came unerringly to a small, sandy clearing that was
marred by the black debris of a dozen fires. Here she gathered dry twigs and fashioned them into a tiny pyre, fumbling in the pocket of her riding-skirt for matches and getting the fire ablaze. When it was burning to her
satisfaction, she heaped green leaves upon it and shortly a
column of smoke was rising to the sky.

She kept that column building for nearly an hour, and
after that she let the fire die and there was nothing to do
but wait again. But soon a horse came splashing into the
river from the eastern bank, and she ran quickly to part the
fringing bushes, and Ord Wheeler climbed gingerly from
his saddle, his coat thrown over his shoulders cloak-fash-
ion, his movements calculated to favor his left shoulder.

"You're hurt!" Fay cried.

"It's nothing," he said. "Just a flesh wound."

They didn't come to each other, they didn't even
touch hands, yet their locking glances were eloquent of the
deep and abiding affection they had for each other. Fay
stood looking at this broad-shouldered, dark-browed man,

a first fear dissolved but the old one rearing to replace it. Breathlessly she said, "McSwain—?"

"Hung," he muttered and told her how it had been, all of it. At the end, he said, "This gunhawk, this Considine from Texas, turned the tide. I was in no shape for quick thinking; neither were my boys. That street would have been a shambles in ten seconds, if it hadn't turned out that it wasn't an S-5 man who shot me. I don't know how Considine got away from you, Fay, and I don't care. It was damn' lucky he did."

She had heard him out in silence, the color fading from her heart-shaped face. "So your own man was up there on the jail roof lining his sights on you!" she cried aghast. "Don't you see? It proves what I've told you all along! You bought yourself nothing but trouble when you bought McSwain's gun and the guns of his friends. And what about Reeves and Blue and Singleton, the three who are left? Are you going to send them packing?"

"I dunno," he said dismally. "I just don't know. I never had any liking for Limpy McSwain. And I didn't hold with what happened between him and Tom Muller, though Limpy told the story different than the way Skeeter Grimes told it in court. Yet I reckon Grimes told it straight. When they set out to hang Limpy, they were hitting at the Raggedy Pants Pool, the way I figgered it. I was positive that Easy Endicott was eating out of Gus Banning's hand. Now I'm not so sure. Endicott could have put us all to riding the owlhoot after this morning's work, if he'd wanted. He gave me a chance that I maybe didn't have coming."

"But still you'll keep those other gunhawks on the Raggedy Pants payroll. Think, Ord! They hired out to you because of what the Pool had to offer them. And for nothing more! Somebody else came along with a higher bid for at least one of them, and that one tried to kill you and almost set this range ablaze. How can you possibly keep those other three after that?"

A harsh thought drew his mouth to a bitter straightness. "What choice have I got?" he demanded. "This thing isn't finished yet. Endicott's quick thinking and Considine's quick gun-work only postponed what's got to come sooner or later. And so long as Gus Banning keeps a hardcase crew with a ramrod like Poe Munger, I'm needing the guns of men like Reeves and Blue and Singleton."

She said, "Banning isn't so bad. Not really. Oh, Ord, there's so much more to this than we know about! Sometimes I think Poe Munger is the real boss of S-5 and Banning is the hired hand. He's a man who doesn't own all of his own soul—I know that. And sooner or later I'll get my chance to find out why."

Wheeler's eyes lighted. "The office safe—?"

"Not yet," she said. "It's always locked. But if S-5's secret is down on paper, it's in that safe. I need time, Ord. But meanwhile I've got you to worry about."

"I'm sorry," he said.

She sensed the unyielding hardness of him in the way that he spoke, and she turned away then, knowing that all had been said that could be said, knowing that old arguments gathered no fresh force from age. He came after her, putting his arm about her shoulders with a big man's awkwardness and kissing her on the cheek. "You can always come across the river," he reminded her.

"What would that change?" she asked wearily and climbed into the roan's saddle. Without looking back, she guided the mount through the bushes and into the stream, forgetting to hoist her feet in the crossing; and when she came into the willows that crowded down to the water's edge, she sought out a trail automatically and rode along blindly oblivious to her whereabouts. She thought she heard Wheeler call after her, but she wasn't sure, and she didn't turn around. She stayed locked in her lethargy until she almost rode over the man who lay stretched beside the trail, a picture of indolent laziness with his head pillowed on his sombrero, a blade of grass between his teeth. Her own sorrel saddler grazed nearby.

"Howdy," Brad Seldon said with a smile.

"You!" she gasped and remembered that lone rider who'd stirred the dust out of Calumet after the S-5's departure.

"There's one thing that will have to be changed," he said solemnly. "Once we're married, there'll be no more of this meeting other men on yonder island."

Anger brought a blossoming scarlet to her face. "So you add spying to your other accomplishments, Mr. Considine!"

He came to his high, erect stand and carefully brushed himself, the good humor still bubbling in him. "I couldn't help but get a glimpse of Mr. Wheeler, both coming and going, since he angled over to the island and was visible from this bank. But what fetched me here in the first place was that smoke signal. 'Injuns!' I said to myself. Believe me, Miss Abbott, I've one ambition I've cherished since childhood. I've always wanted to ride and warn the settlers that the Indians are coming."

She said, "This isn't Custer's time. There's no reservation within a hundred miles of here, and there hasn't been trouble since Sitting Bull's day."

He spread his hands in a gesture of mock despair, grinning ruefully. "There you go spoiling it!" he complained. "And I had it all pictured—me riding a foam-flecked horse to the fort, arrows sticking out of me till I looked like a porcupine, and then dropping dead at your feet. If that happened, would you cradle my head in your lap, Miss Abbott?"

She said stiffly, "Considine, I wonder if you know how much I hate you and all of your gun-handy breed?" Then, quickly: "How do you know my name?"

"The sheriff recognized your sorrel."

The color left her cheeks. "You told him how you came by it?"

"I spun him a yarn," he admitted. "But don't worry;

he won't come looking for you with his handcuffs. And we'll think up a windy for Gus Banning, too."

"You're going to S-5?"

He shrugged and spoke a wanderer's philosophy. "One place is as good as another, and I need a job. Besides, I had to swap horses with you. He's speedy, that sorrel, but I doubt me if he's long on bottom. Shall we ride? Think of the fun you can have hating me from here to the ranch."

He put his hand to her elbow; her lips drew tight but she came down out of the saddle and crossed over to her own horse, frigidly accepting his help in mounting. When he'd climbed to the roan's kak, they single-filed along the trail and wended a twisted way out of the river bottoms and to the higher land, and almost at once they saw the sprawling buildings of S-5 ahead.

Out of a long silence, Seldon abruptly said, "I suppose Wheeler told you what happened in town. McSwain's got his needings, so you might as well put that thousand dollars you offered me right back in your little tin bank."

She reined to a stop. "I know all the things you must think of me," she said. "You've pegged me for a turncoat who draws the pay of one brand and sides another. I'm beholden to you for what your gun stopped in Calumet this morning, and I could give you the truth about why I wanted McSwain freed. But I don't think you'd understand, Mr. Considine."

He hoisted one shoulder in a gesture that might have meant anything. Giving him a long look, it came to her that at times it was hard to tie his strange and varied personality to the scary tales that went with his name.

She said, "I knew the Raggedy Pants Pool would try to save McSwain, and I also knew that S-5 would be on hand to see that the hanging came off. There were all the makings of a range war, and I wanted to stop it. If McSwain had been released last night, he'd have likely headed out of the basin, and there'd been no need for S-5 men or Pool riders to come with their guns this morning. It was worth every cent I had to keep that from happening. Do you believe me?"

All solemnity, he said, "Yes, I believe you. But that doesn't explain why you stayed behind at Cowper's Ford this morning to keep me from getting to town. But I suppose that was for Ord Wheeler's sake."

"I don't have to tell you why I'm siding Wheeler," she said. "I told you at the ford that the thing I was fighting for was probably lost. Keeping you on ice might have meant one less gun against Ord in Calumet. As it was, it worked out differently. And I'm thanking you for what you did."

"Very well," he said and nodded. "That's the S-5 ahead, I judge. It might be better if you rode on alone. I don't think Banning will go crazy with joy when he sees me, and it might be awkward if it looked like you'd fetched me here."

"That's true," she agreed and touched her spurs to the sorrel. "Good-by, Mr. Considine. I'd like to ask you not to take a job with S-5, but I suppose you're still looking for the highest bidder. Likely you've found him."

He raised his hand in a quick salute, and the laughter came back into his eyes. "So long," he said. "Take care of yourself. And don't go sitting on any logs."

6 : "He Ain't Hush!"

Gus Banning had gone into Calumet to see Limpy Mc-
Swain hanged, and, with that deed accomplished, he came
across Hurumpaw's miles with his crew strung out behind
him and Poe Munger riding at his right side, the pair holding sullenly silent and looking none too pleased with this
day's doings. S-5's men, chosen for capabilities beyond the
use of horse and rope, made small talk, some of them
grumbling aloud and all of them manifesting a deep disappointment in sundry ways. They were men who'd been
keyed to a fight that had not been forthcoming, they
needed the crash of conflict as others needed meat and
drink, and they'd followed a leader who'd failed them. Gus
Banning's name would be used profanely in bunkhouse
talk tonight.

All this Banning knew; he had hired and fired men
most of his mature years, and he'd handpicked these with
an eye to certain qualifications that included the very hair-
trigger tempers that were now turned against him. He
could feel their scorn as he might have felt a toothy wind,
and he knew the run of Poe Munger's thoughts as surely as
though Munger had voiced them. And Munger would call
him to account when the ranch house was reached.

Thus Banning, far less his own master than most men
knew, might have drawn out this return journey to a long
fullness, postponing whatever waited at trail's end and using the gathered minutes to frame some sort of defense for
himself. But Munger set the pace, alternating between a
steady walk and a brisk trot and keeping his squinted eyes

straight ahead; the miles unreeled with monotonous regularity and S-5's buildings soon broke the bleakness to the north.

This S-5 was a sight to take a man's breath away. The nearby river gave it greenness and trees shadowed the sprawling ranch house and flowers freckled the spacious yard. The main building was a low, rambling affair with wings that had been added haphazardly as S-5 expanded, yet the whole had an air of solidity and comfort. Barns and outhouses and corrals made a semicircle behind the ranch house; the cook-shack and bunkhouse would have gladdened a wayfarer's eye; but Banning looked upon all this with none of a master's pride. He stepped down from his saddle wearily before the ranch-yard's gate, and a small golden collie came bounding to give riotous welcome.

"Down, Shep, old boy," Banning said.

Munger led his boss's saddler away, and Banning strode into the cool spaciousness of an arched hallway and to his own roomy office just off of it. An oaken desk centered the office, with scattered chairs to match it; a filing cabinet reared against one wall and an iron safe squatted in the corner. Banning fished a cigar from a box on the desk, clamped the weed between his teeth, and made a spread-legged stand at a wide window facing the west. He could see Munger unsaddling out at the corral, and soon the stoop-shouldered segundo was calling the crew around him and obviously giving them orders for the rest of the day.

Banning crossed the room. Its only picture was a huge, framed enlargement of a photograph taken at some bygone roundup. A dozen men squatted before a chuck-wagon, plates in their laps and tin cups in their hands; and one of them was Gus Banning himself, and another was Cholla Sam Seldon, younger then and able to do a good day's riding. Cholla Sam had a high-boned face, not unlike one Banning had seen in Endicott's office today, but the S-5 boss didn't notice the similarity. Not then. He stood studying Seldon, hiding the run of his thoughts behind a wooden expression; and he was still standing, the cigar burned down to a dead, blackened stub, when Poe Munger came cat-footing into the office a full hour later.

Banning turned around slowly. "Well," he invited. "Say it."

Munger shook his head. "You're the one to do the talking. And you're the bucko who should have spoken in Calumet. The boys were primed to rip into the Raggedy Pants outfit, but they needed your word. Damn it, Gus, why didn't you give it?"

"You heard what Endicott said," Banning retorted with a sudden show of temper. "He'd have outlawed the bunch of us if we'd cracked a cap. This isn't West Texas, Poe, and this isn't the old days. There's law in Hurumpaw. We can't go kicking it around just because we'd like to!"

"So you played it safe," Munger sneered. "Then why in blazes didn't you step in when Wheeler's bunch started throwing lead? Afterward we could have argued that we were siding that same law you're so scared of."

"Like hell, Poe! Wheeler wasn't tossing lead at *us*. And even while Endicott was dodging those bullets, he took time to shout a warning for me to keep out. I tell you he's not fooled much, that Endicott. Did you hear him ask me whether I *wanted* a range war when I jumped him about trying to make a truce with Wheeler?"

"Maybe you're right," Munger said grudgingly and fell to pacing the office. In these long minutes of silence, Banning moved to the room's front window and took a stand; and here he had a glimpse of Fay Abbott when she dismounted before the gate, the collie running to her. The girl gave the golden dog an affectionate hug, then came into the house, her boot heels beating a tattoo down the hallway to her own room.

Frowning, Munger said, "Now where the blazes has she been riding? She's in the saddle half the time."

Banning shrugged. "I've never worked her by the

clock. She's got her ledgers to keep; and so long as they're balanced and ready whenever a report has to go to Cholla Sam, I don't kick. I can't change *everything* around here, Poe."

"She's got her own horse, I see," Munger said after a look through the window. "Yet that damn' Considine had it when he rode into Calumet this morning. Or so one of the boys told me. Did you notice that?"

"I'll ask her about it," Banning promised. "And, by the way, how do you figure this Considine fits into things? He's the man you should be cussing for today's slip, not me. When the bullet hit Ord Wheeler, we had everything the way we wanted it. In a split second the Raggedy Pants boys would have opened a fight, and we'd have had no choice but to give it back to 'em. Even Endicott couldn't have held that against us. But Considine spoiled the play when he spilled that jigger off the jail roof."

"And that was five hundred dollars shot to pieces!" Munger said darkly. "I had to pay that gent in advance, and he probably spent the money long before the sign shaped up to give him his chance at Wheeler. But about this Considine—"

"God!" Banning interjected. "He's stepping out of his saddle at the gate right now!"

Munger came to the window in two long strides, getting his brief glimpse of Seldon's high, somber figure before the black-garbed man disappeared under the porch's awning. The door knocker clanged, and Banning, remembering himself as the master here, went out into the hall. When he'd pulled back the door, Seldon said, "Howdy."

Banning frowned. "What in the devil brings *you* here?" he demanded.

"Do you always talk business on your front doorstep?" Seldon asked pointedly.

"Come in," Banning invited in gruff surrender and led the way to the office. Munger had put his shoulders to the wall, where he leaned with folded arms, saying nothing and acknowledging Seldon's single word of greeting with a curt nod. Banning seated himself behind the desk, leaving Seldon standing, and Banning said, "What does Endicott want now?"

"You'd have to ask him," Seldon said. "I've been my own man since McSwain got his needings."

"You mean Endicott didn't send you?"

"They tell it that you hire men, Banning—the right kind of men. I could use a job."

This startled Banning into a show of surprise. He drummed his fingertips on the desk's smooth surface and took a moment before he said, "What makes you think I'd need your kind?"

"I shoot straight," Seldon said. "You know that. And I can keep my mouth buttoned tight. Isn't that worth something to you?"

"You seem to favor the law."

Seldon shrugged. "Mostly I favor Hush Considine. The sheriff needed a man, and the money sounded good. I was getting low on tobacco. Besides, badge-polishing was a new one on me. That's over. Whoever gets me on their payroll, gets all of me. Do I make myself clear?"

"Clear enough," Banning conceded and became bolder with this frank facing of the cards. Abruptly he said, "Then you'd be my man, even if it meant turning your gun against Easy Endicott himself?"

Seldon made another shrug. "There's nothing owing between me and the sheriff," he said. "When I was his man, I did his bidding. That's finished."

There was now less tension to Banning; he leaned back in his chair and crossed his boots on the desk top and locked his fingers at the nape of his neck.

"I can use you, Considine," he said. "S-5 isn't hard on its men, but some of your duties may be—er—rather unorthodox. You've been in the basin long enough to have got an inkling of the situation here. That situation is bound to build to a showdown. S-5 intends to be law-abiding, of course; but it is often hard to fit old laws to new developments, and circumstances sometimes arise that are better handled by more direct means. I hope you thoroughly understand that."

Seldon yawned. "You tell it pretty," he said. "Don't bother with the rest of the oration. I told you I knew how to keep my lip buttoned."

Banning colored. "If you think—!" he began.

"I don't think," Seldon said, his tone cold. "Let's get that straight. You're the boss, and I'll expect you to do the thinking. When you get it done, let me know what the chores are to be. That's the way you want it, isn't it?"

Banning smiled. "Exactly," he said. "Go out to the bunkhouse. If you aren't packing a turkey, the boys will fix you up with anything you need."

But still Seldon made his stand. "About the pay—?" he queried.

"Fifty a month—and beans and bullets."

Seldon turned toward the door. "Thanks," he said dryly. "I can always make tobacco money. I'm pleased to have met you, Banning. Maybe we'll meet again."

Banning's feet thudded to the floor, and he came up out of the chair. "Wait!" he cried. "How in the devil much do you think you're worth anyway? There's plenty of men who ride for thirty a month and found and call it a square deal."

"Sure," Seldon agreed. "And down in Mexico I've seen peons break their backs all day long under a broiling sun to get a handful of tortillas. They keep happy too, but that doesn't mean *I'm* working for poker chips or cigarette pictures."

"Seventy-five a month," Banning said.

Seldon gave this his silent consideration. Then: "It's a deal," he decided.

He was another step toward the door when Banning said, "Just one more thing. My boys tell me you came into

Calumet this morning on an S-5 horse. I'd like to know about that."

"Oh, the sorrel?" Seldon said. "The little lady loaned it to me. My own needed a rest, and I was in a hurry. She didn't want to swap at first, but when I explained that I was a special deputy, she changed her mind. Your S-5 hands must all be long on that law-abiding spirit, Banning."

He was gone then, the outer door banging after him; and Banning swore softly as he watched that high figure cross the porch and round the building in the direction of the bunkhouse. Turning to Munger, who'd stood silent all this while, he said, "Well, what do you make of him, Poe?"

"He ain't Hush!" Munger said flatly.

Banning jerked as though the swift force of a heavy fist had caught him. "How do you know that?"

"I've had the hunch ever since I saw him in Calumet. It's been growing on me since. I was going to tell you when we first started talking about him, but he came riding up just then. While he palavered with you, I had my eyes on him. I saw Considine once—down in Texas years back. He was pointed out to me in a cantina, but I was loaded to the eyebrows with tequila at the time. I've seen a lot of men since, and I had to sort through the faces. Considine would be an older man, for one thing. This jigger wears the black garb; he talks low and keeps his throat covered. But he ain't Hush Considine!"

Banning began to pace restlessly back and forth across the office's narrowness. "What's his game then?" he suddenly demanded, and at this moment he was completely the underling, leaning on the strength and the cunning of Poe Munger and looking to the man with utter helplessness. "Did Endicott send him here? Is he spying for the sheriff?"

"I don't think so," Munger decided. "From the way town talk sounded this morning, it seems Endicott was taken in by him and hired him because he thought he was getting a hardcase Texican gunhawk. He fooled Easy as bad as he's trying to fool us."

"He didn't seem to care much whether he got a job here," Banning said. "And he held out for higher wages—and got 'em. Maybe that's what's behind his pretense. A two-bit gunman trading on Considine's reputation."

"We've got to know," Munger said slowly. "We've got to know."

"What about the scar?" Banning demanded. "Isn't Considine supposed to have a bullet scar on his throat?"

"And Considine keeps his throat covered night and day. He's mighty touchy about that scar; it can't be a pretty thing to see. This galoot would get suspicious was we to ask for a look or try to sneak one."

"How are we going to tell, then?"

"I think I know," Munger said slowly. "I'll be taking some of the boys for a ride tomorrow night. We've got to stop a train. Yeah, I got the word in town this morning, and I've made my plans. I'll just take this Hush Considine along on that little pasear. If he's some tinhorn gunnie who's borrowed a rep for himself, it won't matter. But if he's here for any sneaking reason of his own, I'll find out. Because I'll figger out a chore to give him that'll force his hand."

Banning sleeved sweat from his face. "But won't that be risky, pal? Suppose he does turn out to be some sort of fake—a lawman working undercover, for instance? He'll know too much about us after that trip."

"Then," said Poe Munger, "he may ride away from S-5 with me—but he won't be riding back."

7 ⦙ **To Stop a Train**

From a day coach's niggardly comfort, Charlie Fenton, free-lance surveying contractor, had watched an unbroken panorama of prairie miles unreel; and now, in the deepening dusk at a long day's ending, he had his glimpse of the Hurumpaws to the west as the rails bent toward those bulking hills. A traveled man, this Fenton never thrilled to the sight of earth's upthrusts; his was a surveyor's mind and all things that were obstacles in the retracing of old lines or the establishing of new ones were obnoxious to him. He was on his way to do one more surveying job, and the Hurumpaws were a challenge to an old man's skill.

Hunched in the coach's seat, Fenton made a small and unobtrusive figure. He had lived full years, he had measured desolation and saw its peopling as the fruit of his work, he had crossed loneliness with compass and flag and chain and stake, and loneliness had ceased to be. All these things had put their mark on him. Weather had browned his dour and homely face, wind had bowed his heavy shoulders, and wetness had put the misery in his bones. He would quit next season—he had made himself that promise across a score of years, yet he knew full well that he'd die at a transit, and his grave would be just one more mark he'd leave behind him.

His crew was with him in the coach, and they comprised all its passengers—compass men and red-shirted flagmen and chainmen and axmen and others who did less-skilled work, a dozen in all. A gay and vociferous party, some played poker on suitcases laid across their knees, others spun tall tales of troublesome surveys on distant ranges, but all of them left Fenton to his silent musings. They had served him long, and they knew that to him a job was a campaign to be planned with a veteran's care.

Yet he was merely dreaming now; and while his dreams ran on, the darkness crowded up against the windows, the lamps stayed unlighted, and the Hurumpaws' outlines were lost in the oblivion of the night until a great full moon came rising. Fenton caught himself dozing, and he dug into the big, waterproof pocket of his light coat for his pipe and tobacco pouch. The pipe stoked, he fumbled again and said, "Anybody got a match?"

Big Dan Courtney, a compass man himself and for many years Fenton's chief assistant, supplied the light and slid into the seat when Fenton nodded an invitation. Courtney said, "What sort of work do you think we'll find on the other side of those hills, chief?"

Fenton hunched a shoulder. "Hard telling. All I've got is the letter that fellow Gary Strawn wrote for some Judge Boaker. Strawn's a county attorney. That means the survey's to straighten out some piddling legal question."

The train had settled to a slow climb into the hills, and Fenton sucked silently on his pipe for many minutes. Then: "It'll be trouble, that's a cinch. A re-survey always is, anyway. We'll lose weeks finding the old starting point, likely. I suppose cattle have rooted up every stake that was driven."

"What about the field notes of the first survey?"

Fenton expelled a cloud of smoke. "Confounded things never are where a man can lay his hands on them," he complained. "Probably went to start a campfire one cold morning. Dan, I've wasted my best years butting my head against the walls built by other men's incompetence."

"We can hope for the best," Courtney said.

Again the silence fell between them. Fenton kept working at his pipe, littering the aisle with borrowed matches and fouling the air; the train reached the first rise of the Hurumpaws and leveled off to cross a high, spider-legged trestle over a wide canyon with moonlight faintly touching the winding ribbon of a creek far below. Fenton stirred with interest; he could appreciate man's conquest of the mountains. He said, "We should be getting into Calumet around midnight."

Two matches later the train slid into a tunnel, the sudden complete darkness swooping down and Fenton's pipe glowing redly, a single eye to light it. One of the poker players said, "Too bad we called off our game. A man could earn his chips easy *now.*" He got his laugh, and somebody came stumbling down the aisle. "Who in blazes is taking a walk at a time like this?" Courtney demanded.

It was the conductor, and he got the lamps aglow and went on to the last coach. There were only the two and a baggage car, and the train crept out of the long tunnel and began its climbing again, but was soon dipping downward, the brakes squalling against the grade. Shortly thereafter the engine eased to a stop; and when the surveying crew began asking questions, Fenton peered through the window into a black chaos of pine and rock, dappled intermittently by moonlight, and made out the squat, high-legged silhouette of a water tank.

"Train's taking on a drink," he grunted.

That was when the man materialized in the coach's doorway and moved to block the aisle, the lath-lean, round-shouldered man with squinted eyes above the bandanna that masked the lower half of his face. He had a gun, the barrel darting like a questing snake, and he said, "Easy, now! All of you!"

"Gawd!" an axman ejaculated. "It's a holdup!"

Charlie Fenton shot to a stand, a coiled spring released for action, his eyes running quickly to the bulky bundles heaped on the empty seats. These held the compass and chains and tally pins, and the equipment for the clerical work that goes with surveying, and there were cases, too, holding the tents and Mackinaw blankets and other camping paraphernalia. Though these things were valuable to the party, they were hardly worth holding up a train to get, and Fenton said, "What the devil do you want?"

"Fenton—Charlie Fenton," said the masked man. "Which one of you is him?"

No one spoke, a heavy silence holding for ten seconds. "Speak up!" the masked man ordered, his voice venomous. "I've friends outside. We'll take the whole bunch of you along, if we have to. We ain't got all night to wait!"

All the judgment of his frontier years told Fenton that here was a man who meant grim business, and he said quietly, "You won't need to bother. I'm Fenton."

The masked man gestured with his gun. "Off!" he ordered.

Fenton came up the aisle, a little man who stood no higher than the masked invader's shoulder, and he brushed past the man with the gun and poised on the steps of the coach. He could see other men strewn out along the grade, three or four of them. The one on the train was speaking again.

"Once this shebang gets rolling," the masked man announced, "you can yank the bell cord and have it stopped. And you can come back looking for us. But don't do it—unless you want to find your boss dead. Got that straight?"

Fenton glanced over his shoulder and caught Dan Courtney's eye. "Do as he says, Dan. That's an order."

Then he stepped off the train.

Brad Seldon had been on S-5's payroll for nearly thirty hours before he was put to work, the elapsed time proving Gus Banning's claim that the spread was easy on its men. Seldon had slept late and breakfasted well this second day, and he had been at the corral when Poe Munger issued orders to the assembled crew. There were fences to be patched and drifted cattle to be turned back from the western hills, but when each man had gotten his assignment, Seldon was still left standing.

"Take it easy, and get in a siesta if you can, feller," Munger told him. "There's a chore for you and me tonight that'll keep us in the saddle long after deep dark."

Seldon had nodded to this advice, but he hadn't taken it. Sleep held no inducement for him, and the siesta was not a habit he had acquired, in spite of his years next door to *mañana* land. The Rangers didn't pay a man to pound his ear. He spent the day lolling about the ranch, ostensibly idling, but keeping his eyes open. The buildings were all well kept, he noticed. When Cholla Sam Seldon made the next tour of inspection of his far-flung holdings, he'd find nothing on S-5 to anger him.

Seldon made friends with the collie, and he hoped for a chance to see Fay Abbott, though there was nothing that he might have talked to her about. He had two glimpses of her during the day; she was apparently kept busy at her ledgers. And when the late afternoon laid its golden bounty upon the basin, Munger came to him. The segundo said, "Saddle up. We're leaving now."

"Where we heading?" Seldon asked lazily.

"You'll find out," Munger said, and ten minutes later the pair of them were riding stirrup to stirrup, putting their backs to S-5's buildings and heading southeast. The heat of the afternoon was still holding when Seldon saw familiar country, and he knew then that they were aimed for Cowper's Ford. Soon they came past that rocky buttress where he'd slept the night before last. He saw the spot where he'd fought Ord Wheeler, and he saw that deadfall log he'd kicked to unseat and disarm Fay. They dipped down over the rise and splashed across the river onto Raggedy Pants land, Munger silent as ever.

Conscious of Munger's frequent glances, Seldon took to studying S-5's foreman, and it came to him that the stoop-shouldered man was eyeing him with an intensity beyond any casual curiosity. Munger didn't trust him, Seldon judged, and yet Munger had brought him along on this mysterious mission. There were potentialities here that in-

terested Seldon, and he fell to speculating upon their outcome.

This was the enemy's domain, but no riders appeared
to challenge them. Munger apparently knew this country
well and was choosing a course that kept them away from
the buildings of the homesteaders. Three times they low-
ered barbed wire to cross fences, and each time Munger
meticulously stapled the wire back into place again, using
his gun as a hammer. The sun dipped behind the western
wall of the basin, the cool shadows stretched in purple
splendor, the two men ate cold meat out of Munger's sad-
dlebag in a clump of trees in the Hurumpaw foothills, and
here they waited until three riders joined them in the gathering dusk.

Seldon knew these three. They were of a size, lanky as
Munger himself, and they were of a common breed. They
had been Limpy McSwain's friends, and they'd ridden into
Calumet with Ord Wheeler to try to save McSwain.
There'd been four of them then, and the fourth had died
beneath Seldon's gun, and he'd never known a moment's
regret for that killing. He watched the trio swing out of
saddles, he watched them greet Munger with as much cor-
diality as their kind ever showed, and he saw their ludicrous surprise as they recognized him.

"It's all right," Munger said. "He's riding for us now."

"But—?" one of them began.

"Damn it, I said it was all right," Munger snapped.
"Do you think he'd be along if I didn't want it that way?
Now let's get loping. If that train should be ahead of time,
we might not make it to the tank."

They all came up into saddles then, and somewhere in
the shadow of the Hurumpaw Hills they reached the railroad track which ran north and south here, skirting the
Hurumpaws after swinging down out of them. Seldon had
come this way when he'd ridden into the basin, and he was
merely retracing his own steps as he followed along with
the others, the party paralleling the embankment wherever

it could, forcing the horses between the rails when other footing was not so certain, climbing, always climbing.

There was little talk; but from the few brief exchanges of words, he learned that the three who'd joined them went by the names of Reeves and Blue and Singleton. They drew Raggedy Pants pay, and yet they now took orders from S-5's segundo. They had come into the basin with Limpy McSwain, but they served the spread that was supposed to have sent McSwain to his death. This made a new and ramified riddle, and Seldon gave up trying to solve it.

The night came quickly, for sunsets are brief in the high country; there was that hour of darkness when they had only the rails to guide them, and then the moon rose up, big and glorious, and the pine-stippled hills took shape and substance, looming awesome and tremendous all around them. Altitude brought its chill; the sweltering heat of the day was a memory to cherish; and Seldon wished for a coat. The moon climbing above them, the air growing thinner, they came at long last to the water tank, and here Munger pulled his little group aside into the thick shadows of a cluster of gnarled pines. The vigil began then, and Seldon ventured his second question since the journey's start. "What are we waiting for?" he asked.

"To stop a train," Munger admitted. Then: "It's time you knew the lay of the job we've got. There'll be a man on the train—a Charlie Fenton. He's coming to Calumet to re-survey the basin. Before he gets started on that chore, I aim to have a talk with him. A talk that'll stick in his memory!"

The rails began a low rumbling, the headlamp of a locomotive soon penciled the darkness, and Munger drew his bandanna up over his nose, Reeves and Singleton and Blue doing likewise. That orange wisp around Seldon's throat would serve no such purpose, so he fished a large bandanna from his hip pocket and made a mask of it. He had studied Hush Considine's habits thoroughly, and this was one of them. Then the train bulked beside them, the engine easing to a stand beneath the water tank.

"Now!" Munger said, low-voiced but with explosive force. "I'll go aboard. We'll handle this quiet, and we'll handle it fast—so fast the train's crew will never know what's going on. But you boys string out and keep your guns handy. I'll want you backing me if anything goes wrong."

Keeping his eye on Munger, Seldon saw the man swing aboard the first passenger coach, and he saw him herd a little man out of the car not many minutes later. The prisoner, Charlie Fenton, stood defiantly beside the grade, Blue and Singleton closing in to keep him under their guns; the train crew, unknowing, finished its work, and the train departed with a jerking of couplings and two sharp blasts of its whistle. Thus in fifteen minutes time it had all happened, and now the mountain's silence was un-sullied by the chuffing of the departed train, and the five masked men stood clustered around the one they'd cap-tured.

"What in hell," Charlie Fenton demanded then, "is the idea?"

Munger slapped him for a gun and, finding none, he said, "You're going to walk the rest of the way into Calumet, mister. It's quite a stretch, but it's mostly down-hill, and it will give you a long night for clear thinking. And here's one idea I want you to get a good holt on. We could 'a' taken you off that train and killed you, instead of letting you go!"

Anger put a hard ring in Fenton's voice. "If this is some kind of horseplay—!"

"It's no joke," Munger interjected. "You've come to re-survey Hurumpaw Basin. We know that. And when you finish your survey, no matter what you find, you're going to report that all of Trinity River runs on S-5 land. Have you got that straight? Then remember it! Because you'll be a dead man if your report doesn't read like that. Just keep thinking about that all the way to Calumet!"

Fenton drew himself straight with all of a small man's dignity. Wordlessly he turned his back to the group, climbed the embankment unchallenged, and began pacing along the ties in their downward tilt.

They watched him go, watched until the shadows had swallowed him, then Singleton jerked his bandanna down off his nose, drew in a long breath and said, "He didn't bluff worth a hoot! He ain't very big, but what there is is all guts! This might have been a good idea—with a different kind of man. But he'll survey the basin the way it should be surveyed, and he'll go straight to the sheriff the minute he hits Calumet!"

"You're right!" Munger said slowly. "You've figgered it right. We didn't bluff him, so we've got to kill him. Maybe the man that takes his place will be easier to handle, especially if there's a dead surveyor in the hills to remind the next one that we mean business."

He drew in his under lip and sank his teeth into it thoughtfully, and inspiration came into his squinted eyes as he glanced at Seldon.

"You wanted gun wages," Munger said. "Here's where you start earning 'em. Take off down the track after that jigger. And when you catch up with him, see that he stops walking. Got that straight, *Mr. Considine?*"

Seldon nodded, but the gesture signified nothing. For just as surely as though he'd overheard that conversation between Gus Banning and Munger in S-5's ranch house, the talk the two had had about him, he recognized this as a test—Munger's way of satisfying the suspicion Munger had evidenced from the first. It gave Seldon the devil's own choice. He could feel the eyes of these four upon him, hard and hostile, and he knew they were waiting for him to make his say.

8 : A Dead Man Riding

Fay Abbott's office was tucked into one of the rear wings of S-5's ranch house; its window gave her a sweeping view of the corrals from her high counter, and thus she'd seen Poe Munger and Brad Seldon saddle up in the late afternoon and ride away from the ranch. Nibbling at the end of her pen, she'd speculated on their mission, but guesswork got her nowhere. Yet she turned back to her ledgers with a vague and troubled feeling, until at last she angrily told herself that she was not concerned with the doings of that black-garbed newcomer of the soft and whispering voice.

She knew, of course, that he was now employed by S-5. Gus Banning had told her to enter Hush Considine's name in the time book, and she'd blinked at the pay the man commanded. Also she'd wondered what Cholla Sam Seldon would think if he knew what percentage of S-5's expenses were allotted to the growing payroll. But likely Cholla Sam would never know. This S-5 kept accurate accounts; it was no shoestring outfit with its expenditures carelessly listed in an old tally book. Cholla Sam insisted on journals and ledgers, fat and lean, yet Cholla Sam was not concerned with details. Monthly reports to him showed the summing up of a bookkeeper's careful work. Sometimes an auditor came around; usually he didn't.

Cholla Sam didn't even know the name of S-5's bookkeeper, which was why Brad Seldon had had no inkling that a girl was employed by the ranch. But Fay knew nothing about Seldon's surprise, of course. To her he was Hush Considine, Texas gunhawk whose six was for sale to the highest bidder. She hated him, just as she hated all his predatory breed—or so she told herself. Yet when she sat down to supper with Gus Banning in S-5's spacious dining room that night, she took cognizance of the fact that Poe Munger was not eating with them—which he usually did—to say, "I saw Poe riding away with that new man. Will they be back tonight?"

"Couldn't say," Banning replied. "Haven't seen much of Munger today."

She wondered, as she'd so often done, who was actually the head man of S-5 and who was the segundo, but she didn't put her curiosity into words. She had been with S-5 for three years; she'd come here even before Poe Munger, who'd drifted out of nowhere, had a talk with Banning, and then replaced an old and able foreman whose knowledge was confined to cows. Munger had been the first of the gun-handy gentry on S-5's payroll; others had come after him, so many that they now comprised the entire crew; Skeeter Grimes, last of the original crew and consequently an alien on the spread he'd served so long, had drawn his time right after McSwain's trial and drifted.

She glanced at Banning, putting a woman's appraisal upon him; and her thought was that his bluff, handsome appearance fitted perfectly into this lavish room with its gleaming silverware and its soft candlelight. In another age, probably, he'd have been a perfect robber baron, a master of a medieval castle who rode hard and entertained often. Now he was giving silent attention to his food, and it was worth it. A Chinese named Ki served both the cook-shack and the ranch house, and he was a heathen with magic in him. But she saw that Banning was actually eating very little, and she fell to speculating about that, too.

Deep in her heart, she liked this big man, and this in spite of a dozen suspicions that had arisen about him within the last few months. He was the perfect employer; he let her handle her work in her own way, as long as it was finished on schedule. He treated her with studied deference, keeping his hands and his eyes off her. Yet she sensed that he could be hard when the need existed, and that he had known violence in years gone by, and that certain explosive qualities still lay latent beneath the exterior he persistently presented to her.

When Ki had brought the dessert, she said, "So Limpy McSwain was hanged yesterday. It's hard to grasp the fact that he's actually dead. I never saw him until the trial, but I still shiver when I remember him."

He said, "Yes," absently.

"Aren't you afraid?"

He hoisted his eyebrows. "Afraid—?"

"Of that threat McSwain made against you and the others after he was sentenced. He said he'd see you hanged as well as the rest."

"Limpy McSwain," he said emphatically, "is dead!"

"And if he weren't?"

He shrugged, his brows knitting together, and he gave her a long and puzzled look.

She drew in her breath sharply. "I watched him when he threatened Strawn and Boaker and Endicott and the deputies," she said. "He had more hate in him than I thought any one human could hold. But I watched him when he threatened you, too. Maybe I'm wrong, Gus. But it seemed to me as though McSwain were acting a part then. He had to include you, since he was blaming S-5 for what was happening to him. But I don't think he meant what he said to you."

Banning came abruptly to his feet, balling his napkin in his fist and dropping it beside his plate. His eyes went from Fay to Ki, who was silently removing dishes, and then back to the girl again.

"Come into my office when you've finished," he said.

She wondered then if she'd said too much, and fear laid a cold hand on her, and the dessert was dust in her mouth. She came down the hallway to his office at the front of the building very soon, and she found him clearing his desk of papers and stuffing them into the squat iron safe. As she stood poised on the threshold, he swung the safe's door shut, crossed over and placed his hands on her shoulders, his eyes locking with hers.

He said, "I didn't want to talk in front of Ki. But I've got to ask a favor of you, Fay: Will you forget what you think you saw in the courtroom?"

She found his quiet insistence more terrifying than a display of anger would have been. "Prob—probably I was mistaken," she stammered.

"That isn't the point. I wouldn't want certain others to be thinking what you're thinking. Do you understand me? It's not much to ask, Fay. And I've done a favor or two for you."

"I haven't forgotten," she said. "I'd still be slinging hash in the Elite Café if you hadn't pitied me and brought me here and taught me this work. I'll never repeat the thing I said to you at the table."

She could feel the stiffness go out of his fingertips, and he dropped his arms to his side. "Very well," he said and managed to smile. "I'll be gone for the rest of the evening. Sorry to leave you alone."

Striding through the doorway, he paused in the hall. "You keep quiet for me; I'll keep quiet for you," he added. "You see. I know about some of those rides to that river island, and the smoke signal and the man it fetches. No, don't be alarmed, Fay. I'm not asking questions. I don't have to. Perhaps we're in the same sort of split stick, girl. Divided loyalties make a hard pack to carry. Good evening."

He was gone then, leaving her standing there with her hand faltering to her throat and her mind seething; and shortly she heard him walking a horse across the yard, and she ran to the window for a look. The full moon was just rising, and she saw him head south toward Calumet town; but before she moved, she gave him time to be long gone, counting to a hundred slowly.

Then she scurried to that squat iron safe, everything forgotten but the one tremendous fact Banning had overlooked in his agitation. Each night he cleared his desk and stuffed his papers into the safe. Each night he spun the dial, and only himself and Cholla Sam Seldon knew the safe's combination. But tonight he'd forgotten. Tonight he'd strode away and left the safe unlocked. And here was a chance she'd hoped to have these many months.

Quite unashamed, she swung back the safe's door and began to paw at the contents. This range had its riddles, and the lives of many men hung in the balance, and part of the mystery of S-5 might be hidden behind this heavy iron door. It was only a chance; she didn't know what she expected to find, but the opportunity was here and might never come again.

At first her search was entirely futile. She came across papers she had seen before in the course of her work, and papers she had never seen but that had no meaning to her. She found duplicate copies of reports that had gone to Cholla Sam, and she found letters that were dull and dry and spoke of cattle and shipments and consignments and prices and other matters of no real interest at the moment. And then she came upon the envelope and the clipping.

They were in the same small drawer, and the clipping interested her because of its many headlines, a journalistic style now going out of vogue. It had been neatly scissored from a newspaper, and it was nearly a full column long; three of its edges were sharp and yellow and brittled by age, the fourth was jagged as though someone had carelessly torn a last paragraph or two from the account. The headlines said, *Desperado to Get His Dues—Lampassa Kid Goes on Trial—Law Will Settle Long Account.*

This shadowy corner was no place for reading such fine and aged print, so she tucked the clipping into her blouse pocket and had a look into the envelope. And suddenly she was reading with avid eagerness, for though the notes she'd found were couched in the language of a profession beyond her understanding, she knew them to be a surveyor's field notes, and she could understand the map of Hurumpaw Basin that went with them, and the meanings of the markings on that map.

Breathlessly she restored the safe's contents to their original unruffled order, and breathlessly she came to her feet and swung the heavy door shut. She spun the dial; tomorrow Banning would conclude that he'd locked it, just as he always had, but the movement was automatic on her part. She held in her hand the means of settling all of Hurumpaw's troubles bloodlessly; she knew now who owned Trinity River, and her first burning thought was to put that information to use at once.

But how? These notes had to go into the hands of a just and honest man, an impartial man who had the power to see that the great right was done. She thought fleetingly of Ord Wheeler, yet these findings, in Wheeler's hands, might be discredited. She thought of many men, townspeople who'd clung to neutrality as the basin blundered toward war, and she remembered the one man—the only man who could help her now—Judge Hiram T. Boaker of Calumet.

Like a sleepwalker she went to the corral and got gear onto her own sorrel saddler. The bunkhouse was aglow with light and alive with sound; most of S-5's crew was at the headquarters, and she came stealthily past the long building, leading her horse and hoping that none of the hands would appear, for she felt as though the very look of her would betray her surging excitement. Before the ranch house, the little collie, Shep, came whining eagerly, but she said, "No, old boy; no moonlight ride tonight." The dog obediently went back into the shadows, and she swung up into the saddle and pointed the horse toward Calumet.

This was a night for riding; the moon spread its silver spray over all the basin, the sage clumps threw long soft shadows, and the breeze was like a caress. But she was mindful that Poe Munger was abroad, and the one called

Hush Considine, and that Gus Banning was also in the saddle. She wanted to meet none of them; she couldn't trust herself to make a casual explanation for this ride; so she chose a long and circuitous route, the miles falling behind her and midnight coming before she reached the town's main street.

A dim light burned in the jail building's cubbyhole office, she noticed, and one of the courthouse windows blazed brightly, but Boaker's chambers were dark. She wondered then if the judge would be gone to bed, and she decided she'd arouse him if he was. This was no matter to wait for the morning now that she'd come all these miles. She rode directly to the low, rambling cottage, finding it swathed in darkness; and she left the sorrel at the gate and mounted to the veranda and thudded at the door. But only echoes gave her answer, and she paused indecisively, shaken by excitement and impatience.

She knew of Boaker's patio to the rear of the house, and she'd heard that he often spent the summer evenings in it. Since she wasn't sure that the sound of her knocking had reached that distant spot, she came down off the veranda and went around the house for a look. And this was where she found Boaker, out here where the moonlight filtered through the eucalyptus tree the judge had so pridefully transplanted and silver and darkness dappled the strewn wicker chairs and the stone outdoor fireplace.

Boaker was here, and her blood chilled at the sight of him, for he was hanging by the neck from the eucalyptus tree, hoisted by a rope which stretched taut over the tree's lowest limb, a rope which a man was tying to the stone fireplace.

Yet that in itself was not the sight that made her heart cease its beating; she was range-born and range-reared, and thus she'd seen violence and death before, and she had a frontier girl's hardiness to sustain her. It was the man who was hanging Boaker who really chained her eyes, the man who had just finished fastening the rope to the fire-place.

He took one startled look at her, that man, and went scurrying off through the bushes that fenced this yard. She heard the thudding of his boots; she heard the creak of saddle leather and the swift rise of hoofbeats as he went riding away. And she fought hard against fainting, for though moonlight and shadow had made a weird mask for him, she was certain he was Limpy McSwain—the same McSwain who'd been sentenced and hanged, and buried in Calumet's cemetery.

9 ⋮ Shadow on the Moon

Limpy McSwain, flesh or phantom, was in Calumet to-night; and McSwain had vanished into the shadows, leaving a hanging man behind him. Such was the incredible fact that forced itself upon Fay Abbott as she stood in Judge Boaker's patio, so horrified that she longed for the oblivion of unconsciousness, even as she tried to keep her knees from buckling. A hate couldn't live beyond the gallows! A man couldn't stretch a hangman's rope and return to hang another! These were the things she told herself as she fought for the strength to stand. These were the thoughts that sustained her, these and the steadying knowledge that Judge Boaker still might be saved if she kept her head.

She got to the stone fireplace, and she got her hands on the rope's end which McSwain had passed around the fireplace and knotted. Frantically she fumbled at those knots, but the weight of Boaker on the rope's other end had drawn them tight. She tried hauling at the rope, hoping to find the strength to hoist Boaker upward enough to allow her slack to work, and she sickened with the realization that her very act was helping choke the life from him. Desperately she wished for a knife, knowing full well she couldn't afford the minutes it might take to find one. Then she saw her way to save him.

There'd been a fire in this stone fireplace earlier in the evening, a blaze built, probably, against the chill that came with the sun's setting. Now there was only a bed of dying embers, but among those embers was a pine knot, part of it unconsumed, the rest a dull red. Heedless of any hurt, she seized this knot, blowing at it and bringing the fire to life, and she pressed the knot against the rope, pressed it there until the stench of burning hemp choked her, and the rope parted and Judge Boaker crashed downward.

He fell as a half-filled grain sack might have fallen and lay heaped and shapeless upon the ground. Running to him, she got his collar open, and she tugged to release that tightened noose. His usually pink and placid face, touched now by the dappling moonlight, was discolored and contorted, his silvery hair tousled; and it came to her that he was doubtless quite dead, had probably been dead all along. Hanging men did an aimless dance upon the air, she'd been told, but he'd been straight and still from the first. Horror came flooding her again, a strength-sapping wave, and then Judge Boaker groaned and stirred feebly.

He was alive! The noose removed, she began chafing his wrists and loosening his clothing, feeling for his pulse intermittently and finding it feeble. She wanted to run for the doctor, but she remembered that the medico's house had been dark when she'd passed it, and she was afraid to leave this stricken oldster for fear the spark of life she valiantly fanned might die away. She could only stay here, doing her poor best, and the minutes marched—ten or twenty of them—and then she heard a man saying, vast astonishment in his voice, "What in thunder's happened here?"

He'd come so quietly that she hadn't been aware of his presence. She glanced up to see him standing beside her, his tall, dark-suited figure blending with the shadows, and by his voice she knew him to be Hurumpaw's county attorney, Gary Strawn. She had her own odd reason for not liking this man; and, an edge of hysteria to her voice, she irrelevantly said, "What brought you here?"

"Business. I'm working late, and I thought the judge might still be up." His voice caught; he'd glimpsed the rope lying like a silvery snake in the moonlight. "What's happened? Who did this?"

"Limpy McSwain," she said.

Kneeling, he gave her a quick, sharp glance, then turned to examining Boaker. His fingers moved methodically, and she heard the sudden intake of his breath. "He needs a doctor," he announced.

"I was afraid to leave him," she explained.

Strawn slid an arm under the inert body, drew up his own knees, and heaved, grunting with the effort, but when he came to a stand, the bulk of Boaker was over one of his shoulders. He headed around the house, Fay trailing him and trying to help with the load and marveling the while at the strength that lay in this Gary Strawn. At the gate she said, "Here's my horse."

"We'd waste time if the mount's skittish," he told her. "I can manage. It's only a step."

They began pacing along the avenue of shadowing cottonwoods, Strawn staggering beneath his burden, Fay still trying to help; and here they met a man strolling toward them, whistling tonelessly between his teeth. Into a patch of moonlight, the fellow stood revealed, a high, cadaverous man with a badge upon his vest—Deputy Sheriff Sid Greenleaf. He stared hard, his whistle trailing away.

"What in hell—?" he began.

"It's Boaker, Sid," Strawn explained. "He's hurt badly. No, I can handle him. I'm heading for Doc Budge's. Find Easy and get him over there, Quick!"

Greenleaf dissolved into the shadows again; the lawyer and the girl toiled onward, Fay running ahead as they neared Budge's cottage. Drumming frantically on the door, she had the medico at the portal, nightgown-clad and with a smoking lamp in his hand, by the time Strawn staggered to the porch.

"This way," Budge said and ushered them to his own disheveled bed.

Boaker stretched out upon the bed, Budge fell to examining him. He was a pudgy, balding little man, this Budge; he'd tended a range's ills for a quarter of a century, and it was significant that he wasted no time with questions. "Strangled bad," he finally said. "But he's breathing, and time will bring him around. Run to the kitchen, girl, and start some water heating. Judge's got a head wound, too. Whoever tried to throttle him, knocked him out first."

That, then, explained why Boaker had appeared dead as he dangled at the rope's end. Hurrying to the rear of the house, Fay stirred up a fire and got water upon it. When she brought a steaming basin into the bedroom, Budge was saying, "Train's late tonight. Asleep or awake, I always hear its whistle. When it gets in, I'll have the judge loaded aboard. The hospital in Helena is the place for him."

Strawn, pacing nervously, gnawed at his mustache. "Poor Boaker!" he mused.

The outer cottage door trembled to a heavy knock, then opened, and Easy Endicott lurched inside, Greenleaf at his heels. The sheriff had drawn his trousers over his nightgown; his eyes were sleepy; and one suspender was in place while the other hung flapping at his side. He said, "What the devil happened to Boaker, Gary?"

Strawn said, "That's what Budge and I have been trying to piece together. He was knocked over the head and then hoisted by a rope around his neck, but he'll live. He certainly couldn't have hung himself—not while he was unconscious."

Framed in the doorway leading from the kitchen, Fay said, "I told you once, Mr. Strawn. Limpy McSwain hanged him."

"McSwain!" Greenleaf echoed.

Strawn's smile mixed pity with derision. "From what she told me coming here, I gather that she found the judge and cut him down. Naturally she's under something of a strain."

"Don't laugh!" Fay cried, all the horror of that first moment in Boaker's patio sweeping over her again. "I found him hanging—yes! And a man was tying the rope to that stone fireplace. I saw him clearly in the moonlight the moment before he ran. It was McSwain, I tell you!" She swayed, water slopping over the rim of the basin she held. "It was him—just as he looked in the courtroom—"

Endicott reached her and lifted the water basin from her fingers. "Steady!" he said. "Steady!"

Strawn frowned. "I'm beginning to believe her!" he said. "By God, if I'm not! Easy, let's take her to where we can do some talking. I want to get to the bottom of this." His glance shifted to Doc Budge. "Need us any more, Doc?"

"You're cluttering up the place," Budge said irritably. "Get out, all of you. I'll get the train crew to help me handle the judge, when the train comes in."

He herded them from the room; and they crowded out onto the porch, Endicott, a ludicrous figure in his hasty state of dress, supporting the reeling girl. Strawn said, "Bring her over to my office. We can talk there."

That one courthouse window still blazed brightly; Fay knew now that it was Strawn's office, and she remembered the lawyer saying that he'd been working late and had come to see Boaker about some legal business. She let herself be escorted up the street to the rusty brick building, and up the echoing stairs to Strawn's office. The door stood ajar; and when the group shouldered into the room, a man broke his nervous pacing to whirl and face them; and Fay, not expecting to find him here, gasped at the sight of Gus Banning.

"Come to talk to you, Strawn," Banning jerked out. "Found the door open and you gone. Figured you'd be back soon. What's all this? What are you doing in town, Fay?"

Strawn said, "I'll break it to you quickly, Banning. Somebody tried to hang Judge Boaker from his own eucalyptus tree tonight. This girl found him. And she swears it was Limpy McSwain who staged the necktie party!"

"God!" Banning said; the color left his face, and he slumped into the closest chair.

Endicott barked, "Have you all gone crazy? McSwain's dead, you damn' fools! No, I'm not calling this girl a liar. She heard the courtroom threat, and she thinks she saw McSwain. Likely she saw somebody who looked like him. Can't you understand that?"

Fay wearily said, "I've told you all there is to tell. Please let me out of here. I'm going home."

Banning came from his chair, most of his composure regained. "I'll take you home. Strawn, the matter I came to see you about can wait."

Strawn said, "Not so fast. There's one little point I'm anxious to clear up. Just what was it, miss, that fetched you into town in the middle of the night to see Judge Boaker?"

Fay almost raised her hand to the pocket that held the field notes she'd taken from Banning's safe, but she remembered herself. "That," she said, "has nothing to do with what happened to the judge."

"Meaning it's none of my business!" Strawn's voice was flat and cold; a stride brought him to her, and he got his hand on her wrist and twisted hard. "You'll talk, damn you!" he insisted. "What did you come to see Boaker about?"

Banning's hand fell on Strawn's shoulder, and Banning jerked hard, bringing the attorney around. "Keep your paws off her, Strawn!" Banning said. "Is that clear?"

Just for an instant S-5's manager stood transformed, a man hard and grim and deadly serious, and that moment was long enough. Strawn said, "I'm sorry. Will you accept my apology, miss? A night like this is enough to set anybody on edge. You may go, if you wish."

She went stumbling from the office, Banning with her, his hand at her elbow. Outside, she said, "My horse is still before Boaker's. Would you get it, Gus? I—I don't want to go back there again."

"Sure," he said, and went striding away. She stood

waiting in the dust of the street's edge, and soon he returned astride his own saddler and leading hers. As they put the town behind them, she heard the westbound train whistling for the Trinity's railroad bridge. She took a last backward look then, wondering if the town would ever seem the same to her again, even by daylight; she had lived through a nightmare and the scars were forever on her.

Banning said, "Just how bad is Boaker?" She gave him an answer and they rode on in silence, the miles falling behind and the moon fading toward the west.

Thus they came at long last to a point not far from where the Trinity's rushing course was broken by that tear-shaped island where she'd held rendezvous with Ord Wheeler; and here Fay drew her mount to a stop and broke the lengthy wordlessness that had lain between them. "I'm crossing the Trinity tonight, Gus," she said. "I'm riding to the Wagonwheel to see Ord—to tell him all that's happened."

Sitting his saddle, Banning made a fine, handsome figure. He said, "Very well. But before you go, I wonder if I dare ask you the same question that was on Strawn's mind? What took you in to see Boaker tonight?"

She'd had the miles for thinking, and all the accumulated suspicions and fears of a long and silent ride burst forth from her now. "And what took you in to see Strawn?" she demanded. "He's never done legal work for S-5, even though he rides to the ranch often enough. And how much time did you *really* spend waiting in his office? You left the ranch long before I did."

His brows drew tight in a puzzled frown. "Just what's on your mind, Fay?"

"Endicott had the one clear mind among the bunch of us," she said. "Endicott knew I couldn't have seen a man who is dead and buried. But I saw someone—someone made up to resemble Limpy McSwain, perhaps. A lot of time elapsed while I was alone with Boaker—a lot more before we reached Strawn's office. Did you change clothes during that time, Gus?"

"Is that what you think?" he asked.

She said, "If I think the other, I'll go crazy. You're about McSwain's build, Gus. The law's standing in your way, keeping you from warring on the Raggedy Pants Pool. Was that your reason for wanting Judge Boaker dead?"

"Reason?" he murmured. "I had more reason than you'll ever know for wanting him alive!"

Touching spurs to his horse, he swung the mount around; and she watched him gallop off in the direction of S-5's sprawling buildings, watched for a long, thoughtful moment. And in the midst of that moment, a cloud wisp crossed the face of the setting moon, and the shadow, magnified, fell broadly upon the basin. And in the sudden darkness, she turned toward the river, seeing here a symbol of the greater shadow that had fallen upon the basin tonight. Shuddering, she rode along.

10 : **Race to the Wagonwheel**

Given a job that entails even a hundred yards of walking, a range-born man will invariably head for his horse. Thus it was with Brad Seldon, who made a choice, standing in the shadow of the railroad's water tank high in the Hurumpaw Hills. For a long moment he'd hesitated, seeing the tension build in Poe Munger and in Reeves and Blue and Singleton, who flanked S-5's foreman. Munger had handed Seldon a chore—and that chore was to overtake and kill Charlie Fenton. Now Munger waited, with no great show of patience, for his answer. Seldon crossed to his mount and swung into the saddle.

"What'll I do with his body?" he asked.

Some of the stiffness went out of Munger's rounded shoulders; yet Seldon, measuring the man's reaction, would have sworn that Munger was disappointed. S-5's foreman said, "Leave it lay beside the roadbed. We'll want it found. That'll give the next surveyor we proposition something to think about."

"Okay," Seldon said.

Forcing his roan between the moon-polished rails, he started following their downward tilt at an easy walk, never looking behind; but by the time he'd glimpsed Fenton's unobtrusive figure, he knew he was out of sight of the others. Fenton, hearing the clip-clop of shod hoofs on the ties, had turned and was waiting, and Seldon, drawing up, kicked his left foot free of the stirrup and nodded to the little surveyor. "Pile on," Seldon ordered.

Fenton, his dour and homely face impassive, gave him

a long look and silently obeyed. Seated behind Seldon, and with the roan jogged into motion again, Fenton said, "Change your plans?"

"Yes," Seldon admitted. "They figger you didn't bluff so good. They sent me to kill you."

Fenton stiffened. Then: "This place ought to be as good as any," he said.

"I reckon," Seldon agreed and got his gun out of the holster that had been cut for just such quick work. He triggered once, firing off into the crowding pine that built a black wall on either side of the grade, the roan twitching slightly as the gun roared.

Grinning, Seldon cased the weapon. "They'll be expecting that," he said. "They'll wait about five minutes for me to return, and another five for good measure. Then they'll get fiddle-footed and come looking. By that time we'll be deep into the timber and far enough away to get up to a gallop without the noise giving us away."

"You're not siding them!" Fenton gasped.

"Now you're catching on," Seldon said, pulling the roan off the rails and down into the black oblivion of the pine. Here the moonlight reached intermittently through the swaying canopy of needles, and he found a trail of sorts and followed it downward. He'd gained a few precious minutes by his ruse, but he knew there'd be a wild race before this night was finished. Munger and those others would come, and they'd cut for sign. That was the inevitable, and he faced it with no show of concern.

Less than a half-hour later, Fenton said, "Listen! Hear 'em? They're into the timber and after us!"

"Look," Seldon said conversationally. "I was born with a compass where my conscience ought to be, and I can find my way back to the tracks. Figgered it best to put trees between us and any lead that might start flying, but if there's a chance that the train might have stopped below and that the crew's out looking for you—"

"Not a chance," Fenton interjected grimly. "I gave my outfit orders. We're on our own."

"Then hang on," Seldon said.

They'd come out of the timber onto a flat and open glade, a wide shelf on the shoulder of the hill. Through an eagle's eye, it might have looked like a tiny strip of desolation; to a man on a horse, with death crowding at his heels, it was nothing to gladden the heart—not when there were only low bushes, and few of them, for shelter. Lifting the roan to a gallop, Seldon began thundering across the strip, and somewhere in the midst of that wild dash, he heard Munger's voice rise shrilly behind him. *"Considine!"* the cry rang out, and the high peak caught it and sent it echoing, and lead began droning.

Glancing behind, Seldon saw the four riders fanning out from the timber, roaring forward and firing as they came. It was seventy yards to the far edge of this shelf and the slope's protection; it was fifty yards, forty yards, and Munger and those others were doing more accurate shooting as they lessened the distance between themselves and the double-burdened roan. Twenty yards—ten yards. . . . Fenton's fingers clawed into Seldon's ribs, and Seldon felt the little surveyor sway. "My arm!" Fenton groaned.

"Hold tight!" Seldon shouted, and they were over the rim and taking a bone-jolting drop. Now the slope swept downward before them; there was sheltering timber again, and they lost themselves in it.

But Munger and his men were still coming, and Fenton was holding on to Seldon with only one hand and having a hard time sticking to the horse. Into another open space, and with a nest of high rocks before him, Seldon reined the roan to a stop, slipped from the saddle and helped Fenton to a feeble stand. They got into the rocks, hauling the horse after them, and here Seldon silently stripped away the surveyor's coat and had a look at his wounded left arm.

"Not bad," Seldon judged. "You're losing blood,

though." He fell to making an awkward pad out of his bandanna and got it tied in place; but as the task was finished, vague forms loomed out beyond their rocky fortress, men's voices blending in low talk, and then the guns began beating once more.

Seldon, his own six in his hand, leveled it across a rock and fired. A horse reared spasmodically and fell pitching, and a man picked himself from the tangle of gear and went running. Seldon said, "Damn it! It was the man I wanted; I never packed a grudge against a horse in my life. But that'll slow 'em a little. Ready to ride, Fenton? Let's get out of here before they spread to sew us up."

Fenton, his dour face chalky in the fading moonlight, nodded. They piled upon the roan, guarding against any incautious, betraying noise, and they came out of the rocks with Seldon's gun to open a path for them. Charging for the protecting timber, they left milling, confused men and rearing horses in their wake. Seldon could hear the strident cursing of Poe Munger, the flurry of hoofs along the back trail; and Seldon put his skill to the task of out-riding and out-maneuvering the pursuit.

Thus they made a mad race beneath the dying moon, coming headlong through tangled timber, threshing through underbrush, and finding trails when luck was with them. They reached the Hurumpaw foothills without Munger's men getting close enough for good gunwork, and they got into the flat country that sloped gently downward to the Trinity, and now the moonlight was gone and Seldon was thankful for the hugging darkness. Fenton was swaying again, and when Seldon put a frantic question to him, the surveyor said, "Bleeding—bandage slipped—"

Seldon said, "I'll get you to where that arm can be taken care of."

He didn't know how he was going to do it. Calumet lay too many miles to the southwest; it was Seldon's guess that they were now on Raggedy Pants holdings, somewhere almost due east of the little island in the Trinity. Munger and his men had undoubtedly fanned out; Munger would spread his force to keep his quarry from Calumet, their natural destination. But there were ranches scattered through this country, and Seldon now knew he'd have to reach one. He was an alien here, a man who'd stood against the Pool in Calumet. Yet there was Fenton to think about, and a gun could give the orders if persuasion failed.

He was riding recklessly, blindly, keeping a steady course to the west, and, in this darkness before the dawn, he had no true knowledge of his whereabouts. He wondered dismally how many ranches he'd already passed. He pressed onward, mindful that Fenton was growing weaker, mindful that Munger might still be on the trail. He had one hand on Fenton's right wrist, holding the surveyor to him, when a dog began barking and a fence reared before him; and he slipped from the saddle, stiff-legged and worn, helped Fenton down, and found himself fumbling at a gate.

The new day was beginning to creep over the Hurumpaws, and he made out a huge wagon wheel surmounting the gate, but that carried no meaning to him. A saddler stomped in a nearby corral; Seldon thought he recognized the horse, but he wasn't sure. He crossed a rocky ranch yard, supporting Fenton; and he was almost to a crude shack that loomed before him when its door sprang open, revealing a rectangle of lamplight that was blocked by Ord Wheeler's big form.

Wheeler had a gun in his hand, and he held it at hip level. "Considine!" he snapped. "What the devil are you doing here?"

Sharp and compelling savagery in his voice, Seldon said, "I've got a man here with blood on him! Are you going to stand there asking fool questions?"

"A man? Who?"

"Charlie Fenton. The fellow who's come to re-survey Hurumpaw Basin. He's wounded."

Wheeler's gun arm sagged. "Bring him in."

Seldon got the little surveyor into the shack. The

structure had only one room and a sleeping-lean-to; there was a rusty cooking range, a crude table, and a scattering of chairs, and there was a cot in one corner. Seldon stretched Fenton out upon the cot, and Fay Abbott moved from a stand beside the far wall, and Seldon realized then that it was her horse he'd seen in the corral.

"His arm!" Fay cried, her eyes moving to Fenton. "Quick, Ord! Lift that kettle from the stove, and get me iodine and something I can use for a decent bandage."

Smiling, Seldon dryly said, "You're quite a way from S-5."

"So are you!" she snapped.

"I've resigned from that outfit. Worked myself out of a job tonight."

She brushed past him to fill a basin from a steaming kettle; she took the clean white shirt Wheeler fetched her and methodically began tearing it into strips. She worked with a cool efficiency that brought a new respect into Seldon's eyes. He stood watching her until he felt the impact of Wheeler's scrutiny. The Raggedy Pants leader obviously wasn't long out of bed; he was fully dressed, but his clothes were disheveled as though he'd hastily donned them.

Wheeler said, "Fay told me you left S-5 with Munger late yesterday afternoon. Now you show up here with a surveyor. I'd like to know how that adds up."

Seldon shrugged. "Munger took the little jigger off a train up at the water tank. He tried to bluff him into surveying the basin so that the Trinity flowed on S-5 land. Fenton didn't bluff. So Munger sent me to kill him."

"Don't tell me that job was too strong for *your* stomach!"

"Can you savvy that a man can be a gunslinger and still not be a killer?" Seldon said. "The fellow I knocked off the jail roof in Calumet had a gun in his hand and a chance to use it."

Wheeler flushed. "You're reminding me that I owe you my life, eh? Okay. You're free to walk out yonder door with your hide whole, and that squares up. You'd better get going, Considine."

From the cot where Fay bent over him, Fenton said, "If he goes, I go with him. I don't know what kind of mess you've got boiling in this basin; but I know that this man out-thought, out-rode, and out-shot four men to save my hide tonight!"

"Four men?" Wheeler showed his astonishment.

"Reeves and Blue and Singleton were with Munger and me," Seldon said. "Remember that, Wheeler, the next time you write a Raggedy Pants paycheck for those three."

Fay cried, "Ord, didn't I tell you it would be that way?"

Wheeler drew his brows together. "You'd have no reason to lie about them, Considine. I don't savvy just how you stand, but I reckon it doesn't matter anyway. S-5's whipped, if Banning's got sense enough to give up a lost fight. You can tell him so, if you're heading back to S-5. Fay found the field notes of the original survey of the basin."

Fenton stirred with sudden interest. "Let's see them."

Fay gave Wheeler a quick, questioning glance, and he nodded. She produced the papers and handed them to Fenton, moving the lamp closer. Seldon, unchallenged, stepped toward the cot and had a look over Fenton's shoulder. Like Fay, who'd first seen these notes, Seldon had no understanding of their language; but he, too, could see the meaning in the rough map of Hurumpaw Basin that went with them. His eyes widening, he drew in his breath sharply.

"So that's it!" he said. "The east border of S-5 isn't the Trinity after all!"

"No," Wheeler said with grim satisfaction. "It's a line running straight north almost directly from Calumet and cutting diagonally across the river, since the Trinity runs out of the northwest down to the southeast. That means S-5 owns land on both sides of the Trinity in the northwest corner of the basin, but it also means that the Pool has got a claim on land on both banks of the southeast corner. There can't be any fight for water now! The upper Trinity is entirely on S-5 land, but the Pool owns all of the lower river."

"I see," Seldon mused. "Probably there was no other spread hereabouts but S-5 when the survey was made. Banning used the Trinity as a boundary to save himself the bother of putting up fence. That cut him off from acreage he might have used in the north, but it gave him extra acreage in the south. Since there was nobody to dispute him, it didn't matter."

"I've got my starting point now," Fenton said with professional satisfaction. "I'll make this survey in record time." He shuffled through the papers. "What's this newspaper clipping?" he asked.

The clipping drifted from his fingers to the floor, and Seldon picked it up and glanced at it. "Seems to be an account of the arrest of some fellow called the Lampassa Kid, and a prediction that his trial will get him a long prison stretch," he observed. "Sounds like they had everything in the book against him, short of murder. Train-robbing, rustling—" His eyes turned thoughtful. "The Lampassa Kid," he murmured. "I've heard that name somewhere, but I can't quite place it. Where did you get this, Fay?"

"Out of Gus Banning's safe," she said defiantly. "Along with the field notes."

"The notes were probably given to S-5 by the original surveyor," Seldon guessed. "Banning had his own reasons, obviously, for keeping them hid. But if they're to be put to any real use, the law should have them. How about turning them over to Judge Boaker?"

"Somebody," Ord Wheeler said, "almost hanged Boaker in Calumet last night."

That brought Seldon swinging on his heel, a man taut and alarmed. "Boaker hurt! Tell me about it!"

"Go ahead, Fay," Wheeler said.

She began her tale, telling of the ride into Calumet, and the reason for it, and of the spectacle she'd witnessed in Boaker's patio. She spared no detail, yet when she'd finished, he broke his own intent silence to say, "Now tell it again. Tell me everything Strawn said, and Greenleaf and the sheriff, and Banning, in Strawn's office afterward. There may be some little thing that will help make sense."

Bewildered, she obeyed him, going over the account again; and when she'd finished, he stood in thoughtful silence. Then: "I'll be riding to Calumet. I want to see Boaker if he wasn't put on the train."

Fenton said, "Likely you'll find my crew in town. Ask for Dan Courtney and send him here. Tell him to bring the crew and equipment along. I'll be ready for work by another sunup."

Nodding, Seldon strode through the doorway and out to the gate with the emblem of Wheeler's Wagonwheel brand above it. His weariness of body hit him there; he paused with one hand on the saddle horn, gathering the strength to mount, and Fay caught up with him. She said, "You're dead tired! Rest awhile before you ride. I'll speak to Ord—"

He said, "I can't afford to rest. When I saw that map, I thought all Hurumpaw's troubles were over. When you told me about Boaker, I knew different. That map is the key to peace, but only if there's Boaker's kind of law to back it. I've got to get to the bottom of this. Tell me, Fay; did you try bribing any other man but me to save McSwain from hanging?"

She countered his question with one of her own. "Who are you?" she asked.

It came to him that he had no further need for this impersonation of Hush Considine. He had used it to get his job at S-5, but he had forfeited that job by saving Charlie Fenton's life. And it came to him also that he wanted this girl's respect and understanding, and that he could have her trust, perhaps, by speaking the simple truth. But he had to remember that speaking to her might be like telling Ord Wheeler. Till the last card was faced, he could trust nobody; and that locked his tongue.

"One name's as good as another, Fay," he said. "Put it this way. You're trying to keep this basin from riding to war. I'm trying to do the same thing. You'll have to take my word for it."

She gave him a long and appraising stare. "Good luck," she said. "Yes, I did try to bribe another to free Limpy, and he agreed to try. Deputy Sheriff Sid Greenleaf."

"Thanks," he said and hoisted himself into the saddle and turned wearily toward distant Calumet.

11 :⋮: **Man Afraid**

Seldon forded the Trinity where the little island broke the river's swiftness, and he angled southward across S-5's acres with an eye out for Munger and his men. Mist lay smokily upon the river, the dew bejeweled the grass, the air held the morning's freshness, and meadowlarks gave the dawn a melodious greeting. There was a serenity here that was like a promise of peace; there was no sign of any other rider in the unbroken expanses of grassland. The sun kept its steady climbing and was hot and high when Seldon finally came jogging into Calumet.

He found the way to Doc Budge's cottage by inquiring of a loiterer; and he rode the street's length, a silent figure in black, mindful of the curious eyes upon him, mindful that he was already something of a legend in this town, mindful, too, that Munger might be in Calumet and waiting. Coming to the medico's cottage and dismounting, he got no answer to his persistent knocking. A neighbor woman, thrusting her head from her own doorway, said, "Doc took the train down to Helena last night with Judge Boaker. Ain't you heard what happened?"

"I heard," he said and went back to his horse and led the roan to the livery stable, then walked to the Elite Café for his first meal in many hours.

Feeling less weary once the food was in him, he came along the boardwalk to the Silverbow Hotel. A dozen men sat on the porch chairs, their feet propped upon the railing, a tight-mouthed group whose garb was alien to this range. Charlie Fenton had worn a coat such as several of them wore, and suddenly Seldon knew them for who they were. Pausing, he said, "Which one of you is Dan Courtney?"

The biggest among them came out of his chair, "Who's interested, stranger?" he asked.

"Charlie Fenton."

Courtney measured him from those silver spurs that had been wrought in Old Mexico to the flat-crowned, stiff-brimmed sombrero, taking special note of the cutaway holster and the gun that rode in it, and he truculently said, "You'll have a ransom note in your pocket, likely."

Seldon smiled. "Now who'd pay money for Fenton's withered old carcass?" he asked. "Get the directions to Ord Wheeler's Wagonwheel spread, hire some wagons, and haul your equipment out that way. That's Fenton's order. He's raring to get to work."

Putting his back to Courtney, who began spewing startled questions, Seldon went on his way; but two doors past the Silverbow, he paused before the batwings of a saloon whose faded shingle named it the Staghorn. He wanted to do some thinking; and something about the saloon's spacious coolness, glimpsed from where he stood, was like an invitation. Bobbing through the batwings and crossing the sawdust-sprinkled floor to the bar, he found the patronage skimpy at this hour. A toupeed barkeep dozed behind the mahogany.

"Whisky," Seldon said. "Straight."

The glass in his hand, he had a look at himself in the bar's mirror and decided he could stand a shave. He saw the long rows of bottles, doubled by their own reflection, and he saw a soaped legend crudely printed on the mirror: *Have you written home to your mother lately?* He smiled at that.

Then he fell to musing and his mind ran to Cholla Sam Seldon, who had handed him an assignment, and to Judge Boaker, stricken now, whose letters to Cholla Sam had made that assignment necessary. He remembered

Gary Strawn and Easy Endicott and Sid Greenleaf and Buck Prentiss, those other men who had been threatened by Limpy McSwain and had been afraid. And there was Fay Abbott to think about too, Fay who worked for S-5 and who had opened S-5's safe and helped herself to those surveyor's field notes.

She was a traitor to her salt, Fay was, yet she wanted to stop a range war, and that would be for Sam Seldon's good; and thus, curiously, she was no traitor after all. She made her fight in her own way, and he had to admire her for it. He remembered that clipping then, that ancient account of the capture of the Lampassa Kid, and he tried to fit that name into something coherent in his memory and failed again.

Thoughtfully he said aloud, "Texas—"

He glanced again at that soaped legend on the mirror, *Have you written home to your mother lately?* and, feeling the barkeep's eyes on him, he very solemnly said, "A mighty good idea, friend. A *mighty* good idea."

"Sure," said the barkeep and produced pen and ink and paper from beneath the mahogany and slid these articles along. Seldon took the pen, made a reasonably accurate guess at the date and wrote it down, then carefully spelled out the name and address of his Ranger captain in distant Texas.

Dear Captain, he then wrote. *I'd appreciate it if you'd dig into the records and see if you can find me anything on a certain Lampassa Kid. I've got it in the back of my head that he pawed up a considerable chunk of sod down that way a long time ago. Maybe I'm wrong.*

He paused indecisively, then added, *You can send your answer to Hush Considine, care of General Delivery, Calumet, Montana. I haven't finished playing out my string on this deal yet.*

The envelope addressed and sealed, he slid the writing materials toward the barkeep who, finding a common kinship upon which talk could be built, said, "She'll be mighty glad to get that, I reckon."

"She'll cry in her whiskers," Seldon said and laid a four-bit piece upon the bar. "Have a drink on her."

He was turning away when the batwings creaked and Sid Greenleaf came across the floor; the deputy took a stand at the bar and said, "Whisky!" His voice hoarse, he was a man oblivious to his surroundings. The drink poured, Greenleaf tilted it as though he were taking bitter medicine, gulping it down and letting some spill upon his chin and vest. Seldon stepped toward him and put his hand on Greenleaf's shoulder, and with that slight pressure the deputy whirled around, his cadaverous face pale; and Seldon, catching the full reek of the man's breath, knew that Greenleaf was not a little drunk.

"I want to talk to you," Seldon said flatly. "Outside."

For a moment Greenleaf bristled, drawing himself up to his full height. Then he said, "Sure. Sure."

"This way." Seldon got Greenleaf's elbow and steered him toward the saloon's rear door.

Through it, they both blinked at the sudden transition from semidarkness to the blaze of this summer afternoon, and they came to a stand in the littered alleyway, Greenleaf half-leaning against a barrel of debris, folding his arms and taking the pose of a man accustomed to the queer requests of others. "What's on your mind?"

"A thousand dollars," Seldon said without prelude. "A thousand dollars you earned but haven't collected yet. I'd like to know how you did it."

"A thousand dollars—?"

"Don't stall!" Seldon gritted, and he wrapped his left hand in Greenleaf's vest and twisted hard. "It's not so long ago that you've forgotten! We'll not mention the little lady's name, but you know who I mean. She offered you a thousand dollars to make sure that Limpy McSwain didn't get his neck stretched. How did you save him, Greenleaf?"

All the surety went out of Greenleaf, his pretense dis-

A Fair Deal No Matter How You Cut The Cards!

1. Get *Sackett* FREE! It's the Collector's Edition. And it's yours to keep no matter what!
2. FREE! The latest Louis L'Amour Wall Calendar with exciting, full-color art.
3. RISK FREE PREVIEW! Get *Flint* free to read and enjoy for 15 days. There's no obligation to buy!
4. Always Great Value! Keep only the books you want. Build your Western adventure collection one book at a time!

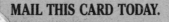

Stake your claim to this free book offer. Send for your Collector's Edition of *Sackett, and* your free Louis L'Amour wall calendar. Try the Louis L'Amour Collection with *no obligation.* See details inside.

DETACH HERE BEFORE MAILING.

FREE BOOK OFFER

BUSINESS REPLY MAIL

FIRST CLASS   PERMIT NO. 2154   HICKSVILLE, NY

POSTAGE WILL BE PAID BY ADDRESSEE

The Louis L'Amour Collection

Bantam Doubleday Dell Direct
PO Box 956
Hicksville NY 11802-9829

NO POSTAGE
NECESSARY
IF MAILED
IN THE
UNITED STATES

solving as ice would have dissolved under such a sun as today's. He said, "So help me, Considine, I didn't do it! McSwain's dead, damn it! Yes, she came to me and made an offer, and I wanted that thousand—wanted it bad. But I didn't do it!"

"What didn't you do?"

"Lengthen the hangrope. That's the scheme I had in mind. There was no getting Limpy out of the jail that last night, and I told her so! Between Prentiss, Endicott, and me, there was to be at least one of us on guard till the gallows got him. If Limpy had got loose while I was supposed to be watching, it would have been too bad. But the rope was the answer. It was long enough to let Limpy drop through the gallows's trapdoor, but it wasn't so long that he'd hit the ground below."

"I see," Seldon said slowly. "And you were going to use a longer rope. If it was measured right, it would look to watchers as though it had drawn tight and Limpy was dangling out of sight on the other end of it. But you were going to give him a nice, safe drop to the ground beneath the platform."

"That was the idea," Greenleaf babbled. "Once everybody thought Limpy was dead, they wouldn't be watching close. All I'd 'a' had to do was make sure it was me who got the job of loading Limpy in a coffin. I could have buried some junk iron, let Limpy get away, and earned that thousand easy."

"And that's how you did it!" Seldon said. "And a good man is maybe dying on the train to Helena because you fixed it so's that kill-crazy cripple could ride again—!"

"But I didn't!" Greenleaf insisted. "I never had a chance to change ropes; Easy kept me busy right up till the last minute. And I got nicked in that fight at the gallows, remember? It was Buck Prentiss who tended to the burying of Limpy, not me. Limpy's dead! Go ask Buck, if you don't believe me!"

It came to Seldon then that this man was telling the

truth, and the proof was that Sid Greenleaf was a man desperately afraid, a man with a fear so horrible that it had reduced him to driveling impotency and sent him to the bottle for solace. And the core of Greenleaf's fear was that the deputy, truly believing McSwain to be dead, nevertheless knew that McSwain had ridden last night and might ride again. That was the size of it, and Seldon shoved Greenleaf hard against the barrel and said, "I'll see Buck Prentiss. And I'll be back looking for you, mister, if I find reason to think you're lying!"

He strode up the alleyway, never looking back at Greenleaf but sensing that the man still stood, unmoving, beside the garbage barrel. He came between two buildings to the street and angled over to the jail building and into the cubbyhole office where he found Easy Endicott plowing through correspondence at his desk and Buck Prentiss, a chair tilted against the wall, stolidly working at his fingernails with a Barlow knife. Seldon had wanted to see Prentiss alone; so he said, "Howdy," put his shoulders to the door's frame, and built himself a smoke.

Endicott looked up from his work with a frown, then bluntly said, "I've been wondering about you lately, Considine. You were headed for S-5 the last time I saw you. Riding for that outfit?"

"Mostly, I'm riding for Hush Considine. Why?"

"Where were you last night?"

Seldon shrugged. "That's a long time ago, but it seems like I was up in the Hurumpaw Hills."

Endicott reared out of his chair. "The midnight train pulled in with a surveying crew that Judge Boaker sent for. One of that crew was missing—the head man—taken from the train at the water tank. Right now I should be out with a posse looking for him. But I reckon whoever's got him will shortly be making the next move—sending a ransom note likely. You didn't go into the hills to stop a train, did you, Considine?"

Seldon smiled. "Now, Sheriff, what in thunder would I

do with a train if I did stop one? But speaking about surveyors, what would you do, Easy, if somebody handed you the findings of the original survey and they showed that the Trinity belonged to both factions? Would you go spreading olive branches around?"

"I'd throw that survey in the wastebasket," Endicott snorted. "What I'm interested in is the *new* survey—and the man who's supposed to make it. But what do you know about surveys, new or old? I'm thinkin'—!"

Seldon's smile broadened. "Take a look out the window, Easy. See that string of wagons heading up the street? Looks like the surveying crew is on its way to do a job. Now here's a tip for you. Just follow them, and you'll find your missing man."

Endicott jerked his eyes from Seldon, had a glance through the window, looked fleetingly at Seldon again, then jammed his sombrero down hard and started for the door. When he was gone, Seldon lazily said, "Sheriff seems to be in something of a lather today, Buck. But it's you I came to see anyway. Tell me, what really happened to Limpy McSwain the day we thought we hanged him?"

He'd chosen this mild approach because he liked this squat, powerfully built little deputy, had liked him from their first meeting, just as he'd instinctively felt a certain distrust of Sid Greenleaf. He sensed that Prentiss liked him, too. The deputy solemnly put his knife away, came to a stand, and said, "Let's go for a walk, Considine."

Prentiss leading the way, they came out of the jail building and angled around the courthouse and struck off across the flats behind the brick building until they came to a small plot of ground with a low picket fence around it, the town's cemetery. Through the gate, Prentiss wended his way among the graves until he came to one comparatively new, its pine headboard bearing Limpy McSwain's name.

"You'll find Limpy about six feet straight down," Prentiss said. "I know, Hush. I took the rope off his neck, and I put him in a pine box and screwed down the lid. Sid was getting himself doctored that morning, and I had all the digging and work to do. Limpy's dead and buried."

"You're sure, Buck?"

Prentiss said, "I take it you've heard the talk of this town today. And I can savvy why you're interested; Limpy threatened your neck, too, that last day. But the girl only *thought* she saw Limpy. If I believed for one second that she was seeing straight, I'd have been out here this morning doing some digging to make sure it wasn't *me* who'd gone crazy. It wasn't worth the bother. Limpy's down below—because I put him there."

"That's good enough for me," Seldon said and turned away from the grave. When he got into the town's street again, he crossed to the post office and dropped the letter to Texas into a slot. Fifteen minutes later he was in the saddle and putting his back to Calumet. He had hoped that Easy Endicott, hearing of the old survey, would work for immediate peace in the basin; and he'd been disappointed. He had come to Calumet with a theory about Limpy Mc-Swain; and that theory had proved to have no substance.

12 • Munger's Move

Sleeping that night beneath the rocky buttress that shadowed Cowper's Ford, Seldon kept his gun at his fingertips, a man acutely aware that he was now an outcast. S-5 would have none of him, he knew; to show himself at the ranch would be to invite the vengeance of Poe Munger. Nor would the Raggedy Pants Pool offer him sanctuary; they'd remember him as the man who'd helped hang Limpy McSwain and had later ridden for Banning. And even the law of Calumet, still making a neutral stand, distrusted him. Seldon hadn't forgotten the suspicious questions Easy Endicott had put to him when a surveyor had disappeared from a train and a dead man had taken to riding.

Thus he was a man alone, and no nearer to righting whatever was wrong in Hurumpaw Basin than the day he'd first ridden into Calumet. Now, indeed, the situation was made more complicated by the tragedy that had struck at Judge Boaker and the weird mystery that attended that tragedy. But at least there was one ray of light. Charlie Fenton was here to re-survey the basin. If the old survey proved to be correct, there'd be no cause for a range war. But Seldon basked under no delusion. The force that had once posted a killer on Calumet's jail roof intended to have a war, regardless.

He'd thought of riding to S-5, proclaiming himself to be Brad Seldon, and acting accordingly thereafter, but he decided against such a move. His identity was his hole card; instinct whispered to save it for a greater crisis. Another dawn found him in the saddle again, a man with no trail to travel; but once onto the flat desolation north of the town, he spied something that hadn't been there before —a scattering of tents and wagons. Riding that way, he found the surveying crew starting its day's work, Charlie Fenton among them, his left arm in a sling.

"Howdy," Seldon said.

"Want to talk to you," Fenton told him, his weathered face revealing nothing.

A score of paces apart from the others, Fenton said, "The sheriff followed my boys out to the Wagonwheel yesterday. He asked me a lot of questions, wanted me to file charges against whoever took me off the train. I told him he was mistaken; said I got tired of riding and decided to pile off the train and walk to town."

Seldon grinned. "I'll bet that left Easy fit for tying," he said. Then: "Why the windy, Fenton?"

The little surveyor scowled. "You mentioned names out at Wheeler's place yesterday morning," he said. "I know you're called Hush Considine, and those other four were Munger, Reeves, Blue, and Singleton. The point is that you were with them at the start. The sheriff might have dusted out five cells, instead of four."

"So you kept the truth from him," Seldon said. "You're beholden to me?"

"You saved my life," Fenton admitted. "I'm not forgetting. But get this straight, mister. I'm not involving myself in anybody's troubles. I'm here to re-survey an old line as per a contract I've taken. I'll run that line, even if it cuts through the middle of somebody's house. So long. I'm burning daylight."

Very solemnly Seldon said, "You've hired yourself a man."

Fenton spun on his heel. "You a surveyor?"

"I can walk a straight line up to the fifth shot of rotgut," Seldon declared. "Give me a job, Fenton. Haven't you heard that the devil finds work for idle hands to do?"

Fenton did a minute's debating. "All right," he said. "I can use you."

And so it was that Brad Seldon, known as Hush Considine, became part of Charlie Fenton's surveying crew. He sensed that this survey was going to provide the basin with its lull before the storm, that all of Hurumpaw's factions would await the outcome of Fenton's findings and then act accordingly. He wanted to see the survey put through promptly, and he wanted to be where he could watch it develop. He was utterly useless the first few days, but he learned quickly.

He found here an efficiency far above anything in his experience. He learned the difference between a solar compass and a tally pin; he learned the function of the deputy surveyor and the red-shirted flagman, he came to know that an axman and a moundman were one and the same, depending on the terrain. His assumed name went beneath the oath that Fenton carried written in the front of his book of field notes, the oath that all surveyors take, the promise to faithfully discharge duties.

He grew to relish this life as the days marched onward; he liked the evening campfire hour when the crew pulled at its pipes and Fenton meticulously re-copied the rough draft of the day's field notes. Here Seldon found the same camaraderie he had known when his Ranger outfit had sprawled beside distant campfires, the red Rio moon above them, the night soft and whispering. In spite of the silent role he'd assumed, he was intensely gregarious; he liked men and the rough talk of men and the kinship that bound this crew.

He soon realized that this was an easy survey, and the finding of the original field notes made it so. Fay Abbott had let Fenton keep those notes; he'd found his starting point at once, and the day never passed but what the dour little surveyor had reason to bless Fay's name.

Campfire tales told of other surveys, of marshy ground and half-frozen lakes, of streams forded and rafted. He heard of tangled terrain where two miles was considered a good day's work, and he marveled, then, at the way Fenton was putting distance behind. He became aware of the time-honored custom of surveyors to let their beards grow until a job was done. He accepted this custom; and he also changed from his black garb to a borrowed wool hat, a large and durable pair of trousers, and a light coat with waterproof pockets—conventional surveyor's clothing.

This was because they were soon high into the land that S-5 had always claimed, and he had no wish to be conspicuous. They saw none of Banning's riders, but sometimes sunlight flashed on field glasses from high bluffs, and they knew they were being watched. Banning would want him dead, Seldon judged. Banning had let him be initiated into some of the secrets of S-5; Seldon had been allowed to ride with Munger on a lawless mission and then had turned against Munger. A bullet would rectify the error in judgment Gus Banning had made the day he'd hired Hush Considine.

But that bullet didn't come, and Seldon sensed again that this was the lull before the storm. He took a wagon into Calumet one day; his mission was to get a fresh supply of dried beans, rice, and salt pork for the crew. He drew a certain delight out of passing Easy Endicott on the boardwalk and not being recognized by the sheriff. He heard the town's talk as he waited in the mercantile store, and part of it brought a worried and puzzled frown to his bearded face.

Limpy McSwain was dead and buried in Calumet's cemetery. Yet Limpy McSwain was alive and riding, for several reasonably sober men had seen him. He'd appeared by night in the town's darker corners; he'd been seen by moonlight on the flats to the north. He was the same old McSwain of the faded denim shirt, the dirt-glazed Levis, and the shuffling limp; and those who'd accused Fay Abbott of a hysterical delusion now made mental apology. Such was the talk Seldon heard.

He wanted to ask about Judge Boaker but decided

against any show of curiosity. He bided his time and was rewarded, later, when Boaker's name was mentioned by the store's clerks. Doc Budge had returned to Calumet; but Boaker was still in Helena's hospital, it seemed, and was slowly recovering. Boaker had written a letter to Gary Strawn, confirming the story that it had been Limpy McSwain who'd tried to stage a necktie party. McSwain had appeared in the patio, a silent, somber figure. Boaker had had his brief, horrified glimpse of the man, and then McSwain's swinging gun-barrel had snatched away the judge's consciousness and drawn the curtain of oblivion across further events.

Tooling the wagon out of town shortly after that, Seldon glanced toward the post office, thought of the letter from Texas that might possibly be waiting for him, and decided he'd ask for it another day.

Fenton's crew crossed the Trinity a few days later; Seldon was put to work cutting stakes from the timber fringing the river, pointing those stakes and charring them for future use by the crew. Now they were onto land homesteaded by the Raggedy Pants Pool, but once again they were left strictly alone, seeing no riders from the small ranches. They camped that night to the north of the Trinity, and Fenton said, "The rest of this job will be pure routine, boys. I'm satisfied now, beyond all doubt, that the original survey was correct. The dividing line runs straight north and south."

Seldon stirred with interest. "Will you draw it out on a map?" he asked. "And write a letter saying you're sure the finished survey will conform with those findings?"

Fenton scowled. "What for?" he demanded. "I told you I wasn't mixing into anything. Now if you think—!"

"Hold your horses," Seldon mildly advised him. "I talked to a lawman not long ago who said he wouldn't be interested in anything but the new survey. I'd like to turn a map over to him, to give him a chance to know what to expect in this basin when the findings are made public."

Fenton's scowl deepened. In these days of their associ-
ation, Seldon had learned that the man never spoke a
pleasant word to his crew; he used truculence as a constant
cloak for a soft and easy nature, and he fooled no one.
Fenton said, "I'll have the map and letter ready for you
tomorrow morning."

Thus Seldon ended his service with the surveying crew
the next dawn. The letter and map turned over to him as
promised, he went to the crew member who'd been dele-
gated as the day's cook, finding the fellow down on his
knees kneading bread dough upon a canvas mixing-cloth.
From him Seldon borrowed a razor and got the beard from
his face. An hour later, garbed in black again, he was
astride his roan and heading toward Calumet. In his pocket
he carried the key to peace and prosperity for all this basin,
if men were so minded to accept it as such. And he drew
his satisfaction from the thought that there was the law to
back him, once Fenton's findings were put into the law's
hands.

On that same morning, Poe Munger and Gus Banning
stood talking together in S-5's ranch-house office, the
stooped-shouldered foreman as worried as he ever allowed
himself to be, the ranch manager doing most of the listening.

Fay Abbott was in her own office in a rear wing, working at her ledgers. She'd come back to S-5 the morning
after she'd visited Ord Wheeler, and she'd made apology
to Banning. "Last night I accused you of being a killer,"
she'd said. "I was overwrought and forgetful of a thousand
kindnesses that prove you couldn't be the kind of man
who'd masquerade as Limpy McSwain. I'm sorry." The in-
cidents of that fearsome night had never been mentioned
by either of them since.

Out at the corrals, the crew was gathered, awaiting the
day's orders, and Reeves and Blue and Singleton were
among them. These three had followed Munger almost to

Ord Wheeler's doorway the night they'd pursued Seldon and Charlie Fenton down from the Hurumpaws. They'd known then, when they'd seen Seldon's destination, that they'd never draw another dollar of Raggedy Pants pay. S-5 had absorbed them; all pretense was gone.

Frowning, Munger stood at the window. "Those surveyors are beyond the Trinity," he said. "They'll be finished in a few days. I'm getting tired of waiting; but if we're going to play the next hand legal, we've got to wait till they turn in their report."

"I know," Banning said wearily. This last week or so had put new lines in his face. "You'll have your range war for sure then, Poe. The Raggedy Pants outfit will start cheering the minute they discover they own the lower river. But they'll take to oiling guns when you spring your hole card on them."

"We'll be ready," Munger said grimly.

"Poe, does there have to be a range war?"

Banning put the question almost as though it were a spoken thought, intended for nobody's ears, but the words brought Munger swinging around, all truculence. He said, "Gus, if I didn't know that you once owned a man's backbone, I wouldn't believe you were the same gent. What did they do to take all the nerve out of you?"

"We won't go into that," Banning said.

"Sure there's got to be a war," Munger argued. "And when it's over, we'll have the whole basin just like this—" He took a cigar from the box on Banning's desk, held it in his open palm, then slowly closed his long fingers and opened them again to toss the splintered, brown wreckage into a wastebasket.

Banning said, "What about Limpy McSwain?"

Munger snorted. "McSwain's dead! Sure, I know a bunch of fools are running around telling it different. They even say Easy Endicott's beginning to crack; he sleeps with a lighted lamp at his bedside and a scattergun within easy reach. Greenleaf's drinking himself into the shakes, and

Strawn looks like he hasn't had an honest hour's sleep in a month. Somebody's rushing the Halloween season as a joke on the basin."

"Judge Boaker isn't doing any laughing," Banning reminded him. "And neither am I. Limpy McSwain tipped me a wink when he threatened me in court, but I'll bet he's not winking now, if he's still alive. We double-crossed him good and proper, Poe. He won't be forgetting that."

"McSwain's dead!" Munger insisted. "And supposing he isn't? If he's still alive, a bullet will kill him the same as it will any other galoot. Sure we double-crossed him! McSwain came here because we sent for him, him and Blue and Reeves and Singleton, and that other jigger—what's his name?—the one Considine knocked off the jail roof. Ord Wheeler thought he was hiring himself some gun-handy gents, not knowing that that bunch was working for us all along. Then McSwain brushed up against Tom Muller and killed him. Tom being one of the original hands, we hadn't let him in on the truth, and when he found Limpy on S-5 land Tom got mouthy—a bad mistake."

"But we promised Limpy we'd see he didn't hang," Banning interjected. "We had to let the trial come off, otherwise Endicott would have got wise that Limpy was really working for us. Limpy said a lot of things about the law and S-5 at the trial, just to stir up the Pool. But, Munger, we didn't keep Limpy from the gallows like we promised, did we?"

"And you know why," Munger reminded him. "You were supposed to order the crew to start shooting that morning in Calumet, and you didn't because you turned chicken-hearted. But even then we wouldn't have saved Limpy. That wasn't part of the plan. Limpy was getting too big for his own britches. He got the notion that he was entitled to a double share when we divided the basin among us. That's something to remember, Gus. Limpy got his because he was getting too tough. A man turning soft is just as big a menace to our scheme. But Limpy's nothing to worry about. It's Considine, or whoever he is, that's tangling our twine."

"You've seen him again?"

"He's with that surveying crew. What's his game anyway? Since he landed here, he's spoiled every move we've made. First he stopped us from tangling with the Raggedy Pants bunch in town the day of the hanging. Then he snatched Fenton away from us when I sent him to kill that surveyor. Now he's trotting right along with the surveying crew. And I've a hunch he'll be bucking us when we play our hole card!"

"Let him," Banning said.

"Let him—hell!" Munger snapped. "He's worrying me, I tell you. And he's one little worry I'm going to get rid of today, savvy! I'm taking Reeves and Blue and Singleton on a little hunting trip. And we're not coming back till we tack the hide of Mr. Hush Considine on the wall!"

He was a man with an insistent need for action; he would always cut his Gordian knots with one sudden, savage slash; and now that he had made his decision, he moved instantly to put it into effect. Striding out of the ranch house and leaving Banning behind him, he found Blue and Reeves and Singleton and drew them into the shadow of the cook-shack apart from the others and told them of his intentions. They were listening when Ed Reeves said, "Look! That Abbott girl is saddling up. Where's she going so early?"

Frowning, Munger had a look and put a quick speculation on the girl's actions. He came striding across the yard, but Fay was already up in her saddle and jigging her mount. She made a show of leisureliness, but he sensed that she was spurred by an urgent need held tightly in check, and he blocked her way and said, "Where the devil do you think you're going?"

Color brightened her cheeks. "I don't think that's any of your business!" she snapped.

A fierce and heady anger took hold of him, and he grasped one of her wrists and twisted hard. "You were spying while I talked to Gus!" he said. "That's it! You were listening, and now you're riding to warn that soft-talking son! You may fool Banning, but you don't fool me, you double-crossing hussy. I saw your saddler at Wheeler's place the morning we chased Considine to Wheeler's door. And I know that you light a signal fire on the island once in a while. Now get off that horse and get into the house!"

Another man, Gary Strawn, had put his hand on her in just this fashion many nights ago, and there'd been Gus Banning to defend her then. Now Banning was nowhere to be seen, but she had one free hand and she lifted her quirt and brought it down across Munger's face. He let go of her with a howl of anger and pain, instinctively raising his arms to shield himself from a second blow, and she used that moment to sink spurs into her mount and thunder out of the yard.

She looked back once as she made her wild dash. She saw Munger flailing his arms and bellowing orders, and she saw men converging toward the corrals at a fast run. She'd gained some slight start, and she used quirt and spurs ruthlessly to widen the distance between herself and the pursuit that was sure to come.

13 ⋮ Six-Guns Speaking

Coming down out of the north, Seldon paralleled the Trinity's eastern bank and looked for an easy crossing, and with the passing hours, he saw growing sign that a storm was in the making. This day had dawned to sunny splendor, but gathering clouds had turned ominous and black; wind-driven, they piled about the Hurumpaw peaks, and the waste of world beneath them lay in shuddering silence. Memories of earlier days made him wise in the erratic ways of Montana weather; the frowning skies might mean the coming of a summer shower; then again, they could be a prelude to a cloudburst that would turn the draws into running rivers and lift the Trinity to a raging, frothy fury.

He forded the stream just above that little island where he'd once seen Fay Abbott and Ord Wheeler hold rendezvous, and raindrops were spattering as he wended through the willows on the eastern bank. He came up a trail to the first high rise, and he found Fay waiting there, her horse lathered and sweat-streaked, her face taut with the strain of a long, hard ride. Breathlessly, she said, "I saw you across the river from one of the buttes. Two men are following me, and I don't think I've shaken them from the trail. They're out to kill you!"

He reined up close beside her. "Two men!" he echoed. "Who?"

"Ed Reeves and Shag Singleton. They chased me from S-5, and Poe Munger and Blue headed the other direction, over toward the surveyors' camp. Don't you understand? We can't sit here talking! They'll kill you if they find you!"

He'd matched gunsmoke with this same Reeves and Singleton before, and that time there'd been Munger and Blue's bullets to dodge as well, and only a wounded, unarmed Charlie Fenton to side him. But Fay was here now, and that made it different; and although there was much he didn't understand, he sensed that her peril was as great as his own.

He said, "Your horse looks like it's done all the running it's going to do. This rain will wash out any tracks that Reeves and Singleton might be following. Is there a place handy where we could hole up for a spell?"

His easy assurance must have been like a steadying hand, for she calmly said, "There's a cabin about a mile south."

She headed down into the fringing willows, the rain's fury increasing as they rode silently in single file. Seldon felt the rain soak through his clothing, and he was thoroughly drenched by the time they reached the cabin. It stood partially concealed by the willows, a decrepit log affair with its door hanging crazily on one leather hinge. It had been built a score of years before, perhaps as shelter for some prospector who'd ranged into the Hurumpaws. Its origin was lost in antiquity, its builder long forgotten. This much Fay was able to tell Seldon.

"We'll get the horses inside," Seldon suggested. "Then there'll be no sign of us if anybody passes by."

This cabin's interior was almost empty; there was a splintered table which Seldon shoved out of the way, a rusty range, and a tangle of stovepipes. A rat went scurrying to cover, the rain drummed on the leaky roof and spattered in through two paneless windows, one facing the front, one facing the rear. The horses led inside, Seldon hoisted the door around to better cover the opening, then had a look from the front window, seeing a sweep of bush-mottled ground with a few rocky upthrusts, some high enough to shelter a man.

The sweaty, rainy smell of the horses already permeated the place; there was little elbow room, and Fay backed herself into a corner. Grinning, Seldon said, "It ain't much —but it's home. Now tell me what put you to ruining a good horse this morning."

"Munger and Banning were palavering in the office," she said. "I came up the hall to ask Gus about some entries, and I couldn't help but overhear them."

She told the rest of it quickly, the talk she'd heard about Limpy McSwain, Munger's worry about Hush Considine, and Munger's final resolve to rid himself of the man he considered a menace to his plans.

"After I'd quirted him, I rode hard," she explained. "I thought they'd all be after me, but he set Reeves and Singleton on my trail, and he and Blue headed northeast. I could see them from the first bluff I reached."

He'd listened in grave silence; now he said, "I'm beholden to you, Fay. Just why did you come to warn me?"

"Because I changed my mind about you," she frankly admitted. "After you'd ridden away, the morning you brought Fenton to Ord's, Fenton told us about his being kidnapped and how you were sent to kill him and saved him instead. I don't know who or what you are, Hush, but you're no killer. You proved it that night."

Irrelevantly, he said, "You and Ord are in love, aren't you?"

Her surprise was genuine. "In love? Why, no! Ord's my brother."

He stiffened perceptibly. "Your brother! You'll have to come again on that one! How could he be your brother?"

"My half brother, to be exact. That's why he's a Wheeler and I'm an Abbott. Our mother married twice."

He began to laugh, and his laughter was whole-bodied and hearty, and when he'd finished he said, "Do you know, I bet I could lick the whole confounded world this morning!"

She said, "Now I see what you've been thinking all

along, and maybe the rest of the truth will help you understand me—"

He'd stepped to the window; suddenly he bobbed down below the sill, his voice falling to the old, familiar whisper. "Reeves and Singleton—outside!" he husked. "Just piling off their horses. Either they tracked us here, or they're looking for a roof to keep the rain off them, too." Jerking his gun from leather, he laid it across the sill and triggered once, his bullet geysering dirt at the toes of the two lanky men swinging from saddles.

Instantly the pair was darting for shelter; reaching the rocks, they flung themselves behind them, dragging their horses from view. A gun's roar blended with the droning rain, lead thunked against the log wall, and Seldon shouted, "Down, Fay! They've seen me. We're in for a siege!"

Outside, the guns blared again, in unison, then fell silent. "Hey, Considine!" a voice called. "We know it's you! And we've got you sewed up tighter than a pig in a gunnysack. Come out with your hands up!"

"They'll kill you!" Fay cried.

"Come and get me!" Seldon shouted.

"We can wait!" came the reply. "We can even starve you out, if we have to. Show some sense and surrender."

To this Seldon made no answer, and the silence hung, save for the steady drumming of the rain. Munger's men were saving their lead and biding their time, but whenever Seldon edged near the window, he drew a bullet from beyond. Smiling dismally at Fay, he said, "Looks like we may have to set up housekeeping here after all. Say, what was it you started telling me about you and Ord?"

He wanted to take her mind off their predicament, and she seemed to guess his intent. "Talking is one way of killing time," she said. "Where do I start? Ord and I grew up on a Dakota homestead. Those were long, hard years. And they ended in failure."

He nodded, listening as she drew a graphic picture of

a bleak and lonely childhood, and he began to see the twice-widowed woman who had been Fay's mother, the woman who had made the good fight and lost it and earned herself only six feet of Dakota earth as her final reward. He could understand poverty; he had seen it on many ranges. And listening, he had the odd sensation of being removed from this besieged shack; yet part of him remained alert to the constant danger.

"After mother died, Ord and I sold the homestead, split what little money we got, and went our ways," she continued. "I came to Calumet and took a job at the Elite Café. Gus Banning found me there and took a friendly fancy to me. He offered me a job at S-5, he taught me the bookkeeping, and kept me on. And he gave me something for which I'll always be grateful—a decent job and the first real freedom from want I'd ever known."

"You sent for Ord?" he asked.

A bullet came droning from outside; boredom and the misery of a rainy watch were behind it; it found a way through the chinking, but it did no harm. Seldon was instantly soothing the horses. Neither was gun-shy, but a bullet's burn could spread kicking, flailing chaos in this little cabin.

"Yes, I sent for Ord," Fay said when silence descended again. "The eastern side of the Trinity was open for homesteading; I knew the basin, knew Ord could thrive here. Other settlers came, too, and Ord was chosen their leader. Then this trouble between S-5 and the Raggedy Pants Pool started—a little rustling, a little fence cutting, and bad blood on both sides."

"That sort of put you in a split stick."

"I owed loyalty to S-5," Fay admitted. "I've never met Cholla Sam Seldon, the owner, but I've drawn his pay. But I owed loyalty to Ord, too—blood being thicker than water. Banning once said that divided loyalties make a hard pack to tote, and he's right."

"I see," he said. "I'm glad you told me this, Fay. I—"

A sudden flurry of motion outside, a wild stirring of the bushes, and the quick rise of hoofbeats brought him edging to the window, Fay at his side. A rider was just vanishing from view, bending low over his saddle horn and quirting hard. "Singleton!" Fay cried in quick understanding. "Hush, he's gone to fetch help!"

"You're right," Seldon judged. "And with enough men, they'll risk a rush that will root us out of here in a hurry. But there's only one of them left waiting now."

"You're not going outside?"

"I have to, Fay. Here—" He swept off his black sombrero and handed it to her. "I'll ease out that back window. Give me time—while you count to a hundred real slow, say —then hoist this hat above the windowsill. When Reeves shows himself to take a shot at it, I'll be waiting for him."

She didn't try to deter him, proof enough that she understood how desperate their situation would eventually become. She only said, "Be careful, Hush."

He was already sliding his shoulders through the rear window, and he got half his body out of the opening and let himself fall, his hands spread and his shoulders stiffened for the shock. He got to his feet, listened for a long moment, then went on hands and knees into the dripping bushes and began a slow, wide circle that would bring him at an angle to the rocks sheltering Ed Reeves.

This was like maneuvering through a nightmare, each movement might be the betraying one, but at long last he came to a place where he could glimpse, obliquely, the cabin's front window and the sweep of ground before the structure. He was certain Fay had had time to count to a thousand, instead of a hundred, yet he had to wait before his sombrero edged into view.

Even then the silence still held, the dripping, clamorous silence, and then a gun spoke, for Ed Reeves had risen to do his triggering, not where Seldon had expected him to be, but from behind another rock, closer to the cabin.

"Now!" Seldon said beneath his breath and came to a stand, shooting.

His quick motion revealed him; Reeves had time to swivel his gun and release lead that whispered waspishly past Seldon's ear. But Seldon was triggering, too; he sent three shots that blended into a single roar of sound; Reeves came out from behind the rock, staggered slowly in a wide and crazy circle and fell upon his face.

By the time Seldon reached the fallen man, Fay was out of the cabin. "He's dead?" she asked breathlessly, and Seldon nodded. "I suppose I'd better bury him," he said. "There'll be time, I reckon. Singleton will have to go all the way to S-5 for help; if I know that crew, they'll be holed up in the bunkhouse on a day like this."

Shuddering, Fay reached and lifted the gun that had fallen from Reeves's fingers. "I'll keep this," she said. "I'll never be without one from now on."

Silently Seldon began to work at scooping a grave in the riverbank's soft and yielding earth. He had no implement, and he was an hour at the task, and when he'd finished and heaped rocks on the shallow grave, the rain had ceased though the sky was still overcast.

"Come on," he said to Fay. "I'm going to Calumet, and you might as well come with me. Later I'll deliver you to the Wagonwheel. I don't want you riding alone today."

She nodded numbly; she'd been badly shaken by the siege's ending, but when they got up into saddles and began putting the miles behind them, she took to talking again. She had given Seldon her confidence, and he probed her with questions; and she told him much about S-5 and the basin, filling in gaps in his knowledge. He listened intently, recognizing all these things as pieces to a puzzle he had to fit together. Out of many mentioned names, he fastened upon one, and when he had his chance he asked, "Strawn? You say he comes to S-5 often. What do you make of him?"

"I don't know," she replied. "He's a capable lawyer

and his record seems spotless. But Shep doesn't like him, and I can't say that I do. That's silly of me, isn't it? But I could never trust a man that a dog didn't like."

"Shep?" he asked, forgetting.

"The collie at S-5. He always growls at Strawn."

"It's worth remembering," Seldon mused.

They rode with a wary eye to the back trail, but they came unchallenged across the miles. They reached Calumet as the sun slipped behind the western mountain wall, and they rode the street's length toward the jail building. Abreast of the post office, they saw its master twisting a key in the door to close for the night, and the fellow, lifting his eyes, said, "Hey, you're Hush Considine, ain't you? Got a letter for you."

He went back into the building and returned with a letter bearing a Texas postmark. Seldon, who'd sat waiting, shoved the envelope into his pocket, jogged his horse again, and came to a second stop before the jail, slipping from his saddle. "I've saved the good news to the last," he told Fay. "I've got the results of Fenton's re-survey in my pocket, and I'm turning them over to Endicott. Come along and see the look on his face. It means peace for this basin, and he's the man to see that it works out that way."

Her eyes lighted. "The old survey was right?"

"Exactly," he said.

She came into the cubbyhole office with him, and they found Easy Endicott here, but even as Seldon stood in the doorway, he sensed that something was almighty wrong. Endicott stood behind his desk; he'd been busy at emptying drawers, and a litter of paper and personal belongings was heaped before him. He glanced up, a distraught and startled man, and it was Seldon's fleeting thought that the man had grown grayer since he'd last seen him.

"Oh, it's you!" Endicott said. "What is it?"

"I've come from Charlie Fenton, Easy. I've got the results of his new survey."

"You'll have to take them to somebody else," Endicott said. "I'm not sheriff anymore. I've resigned."

"Resigned?"

"Turned in my badge," Endicott snapped, and Seldon suddenly recognized what was behind the man's agitation —fear, stark and undisguised. "But you can't mean that!" Seldon said.

"I do mean it!" Endicott retorted. "I'm leaving the basin tonight—just as fast as I finish up here. Don't look at me like you thought I was crazy! I've had enough! Sure, I laughed at the ones who believed Limpy McSwain was alive and riding. I knew he was dead, because I saw Buck Prentiss bury him. But after what happened last night, I had to be sure, I tell you. I went and opened his grave. It's still open, the way I left it. Go have a look, Considine. Then tell me if you blame me for running!"

"The grave's empty—? Then, mister, I want to see Sid Greenleaf. Where'll I find him?"

"Over at the furniture store, getting fitted out for a coffin! Don't you savvy? That's why I had to have a look in that grave. Sid was found this morning, dangling by the neck from the doorway of the little shack he lived in out at the edge of town. That makes two Limpy's caught up with. I'm not going to be the third. I'll fight any man alive, but I can't swap lead with a living dead man. I'm through!"

Wordlessly Seldon groped and got his fingers on Fay's wrist, and he led her outside into the gathering twilight. "This is fantastic—fantastic," he said. "I've got to have a look for myself."

He headed around the courthouse and toward the cemetery and she followed silently along. They came through the gate and threaded among the graves, the ground soggy underfoot, and Seldon moved unerringly to the one Buck Prentiss had shown him not long ago. When he reached the heaped dirt that Endicott had hoisted, smelling the damp tang of it, he stood staring down into the grave, staring at the coffin that rested below, its lid wrenched away—an empty coffin.

He said, "This can't be—!"

Then he was whirling around as a bullet flicked the brim of his sombrero and another tugged at his sleeve, the red tongues of gun flame licking at him and Fay from beyond the cemetery's gate.

"Munger!" Fay cried and Seldon understood then. Munger must have come riding down from the surveyors' camp and met Shag Singleton somewhere above that besieged cabin on the riverbank. And Munger must have been hard on his quarry's heels all the way into Calumet. Now he had caught up with them in this place where death dwelt, for he was here and Singleton and Blue were with him. The guns were speaking, and Seldon reached for his own six to give them answer.

14 : The Knife

As a place for a gun battle, a graveyard had its distinct disadvantage, Seldon discovered; with only pine headboards to break this plot's bleakness, there was no upthrust high enough to shelter him or Fay, no place to turn for cover. Munger and Singleton and Blue, their first shots fired, had dropped behind the picket fence, flimsy protection against a questing bullet; but the premature dusk of this stormy day helped make them vague blotches, while Seldon and Fay stood starkly silhouetted. Upon these factors, Seldon placed a cool, split-second judgment, then elbowed Fay hard, sending her spilling into Limpy McSwain's grave.

"Down!" he cried and came slipping after her. Sheltered by the grave, he managed to find precarious footing on the empty coffin's edge, and he reared himself high enough to lay two rapid shots before bobbing below the lip of the grave again. That fetched a second barrage from the gunmen near the gate; the low, sighing drone of bullets spent itself, and Seldon smiled grimly and said, "What a place to make a fight!"

Fay nodded. She had a smear of dirt on one cheek, and he would have laughed at that another time. She balanced herself on the rim of the coffin and began kicking with a boot toe at the side of the grave. Guessing her intent too late, Seldon moved to stop her, but she used her improvised firing step to haul herself upward and trigger once with the gun that had belonged to Ed Reeves. Just for an instant she was exposed, and a ready gun beyond the fence speared a bullet that fanned her cheek. Seldon jerked her down roughly; he had kept his head from the beginning of this fight, but now anger made his voice unsteady.

"Don't try that again!" he stormed. "Do you understand me? Don't try that again!" His free hand on her shoulder, he shook her violently. "They're not playing penny-ante, those gents. Do you want to stop a bullet?"

She said, "You're hurting me, Hush."

He took his hand off her; the anger died in him; and because he suddenly realized what had fanned it, he stood abashed and self-conscious, wondering if she had read the reason behind his wild outburst.

"I'm sorry," he said. "But be careful, Fay."

She turned her head to listen attentively for any alien sound. "Munger must be crazy," she said. "Does he think he can shoot us down practically in sight of the town and get away with it? He'll have some accounting to do for this!"

Seldon jerked to attention, seeing a means of salvation in her remark, and he said, "Of course! He was counting on a quick job, and he'd have nailed us with those first shots if the light had been better for shooting! If you want to play Annie Oakley with that gun, start triggering at the sky. Here, take these—" He stripped bullets from his gunbelt and pressed them into her hand. "Make all the racket you can, and we'll have the whole town out here. I think Munger will do a fadeaway before the first of them come running!"

She nodded, her eyes lighting. She began working with the gun, and Seldon hoisted himself for another look, drew a bullet from beyond, and got in a shot of his own. He had the fleeting impression that there were only two men behind the fence now, but he couldn't be sure. One might be circling to get at this grave from a better vantage point. Seldon tried for another look, but the bullets came too thickly. With Fay triggering systematically, gun-thunder beat against his eardrums in the close confines of this grave, but a silence fell as Fay paused to reload, and Poe Munger's voice reached them.

"Come out of there with your hands up, Considine!" the man ordered. "You're a bogged dogie, and you know it!"

Fay grasped Seldon's arm. "Listen! Somebody's coming from town! On the run!"

"Munger, you'd better get moving," Seldon shouted. "The law will be here in a minute."

"I'm the law of Hurumpaw County," Munger retorted. "You're talking to the new sheriff, Considine. And you're under arrest for the murder of Ed Reeves. Now are you coming out, or do I have to get the whole town to help me capture you?"

Seldon heard him in stunned silence; he gazed at Fay blankly and he said, "He's crazy! He must be crazy—" Boot soles still beat beyond; a confused babble of voices rose out there by the cemetery's gate. Fay, her fingers tightening on Seldon's arm, said, "Don't go out! Even if it's true that he's taken Endicott's place, he'll kill you. If he intended arresting you, why didn't he do it in the first place?"

"He won't dare kill me now," Seldon said. "Something's almighty wrong, but at least we got ourselves protection by raising enough racket to fetch the town. Hear those folks? He'll have to play lawman for the time being." He raised his voice. "Is Gary Strawn out there?"

"Here, Considine." It was the lawyer's voice.

"Is Munger really sheriff now?"

"That's right."

Seldon gnawed at his under lip. Then: "What about Fay? She's here with me."

The answer was slow in coming. "We've got nothing against the girl," Munger finally made reply. "Toss out any guns you've got and come with your hands high. You'll be given a fair deal."

Fay cried, "Don't do it! He'll find a way to kill you—I know he will!"

Seldon hefted his gun, gave it a moment's contemplation, then sent it arcing out of the grave. He took Ed Reeves's gun from her fingers and tossed it after his own. That letter from Texas was still in his pocket, and he fished it out and handed it to her.

"Keep this for me," he said in the old, familiar whisper. "They'll search me, and I don't want them to find it. Maybe it's valuable; maybe it isn't. Head for the Wagonwheel once you're sure it's safe to leave town. I'll join you there as soon as I get out of this."

"You'll never get out," she said stonily. "They'll see to that. I'm staying in town, Hush."

Smiling, he said, "Don't worry. I always keep an ace-in-the-hole. You head for Ord's, like I told you to do. They can't make a murder charge stick; but if things stack up against me so that I'm really in a tight, send a telegram to Cholla Sam Seldon at S-1. Just say, 'When a man needs a gun he needs it bad.' Can you remember that? And sign it Brad Seldon."

Her astonishment robbed her of words for a moment, but she managed to say, *"You—?"*

He nodded. "Cholla Sam's nephew. I should have told you long ago, I suppose. I'll tell you the whole of it when I get a chance." Tilting her chin, he bowed his head and kissed her gently. Then he grasped her under the armpits and hoisted her to the lip of the grave. "Let's go," he said. "You don't want to spend all the rest of your life in a coffin, do you?"

Out of the grave, he came toward the gate with his hands upraised, Fay stumbling along beside him, silent and obviously bewildered by his disclosure. A knot of men stood awaiting them; there were Poe Munger and Shag Singleton and Blue, and gathering townspeople, some Seldon had seen before and some who were strangers; and the dark-suited figure of Gary Strawn was prominent among them. Poe Munger, the mark of Fay's quirt upon his face, held the guns that had been tossed from the grave, and he fingered one with grim satisfaction. "Ed Reeves's six," he said. "Strawn, you'll want this for evidence in court."

Fay said, "He'll never come to trial, Munger. And you know it!"

Shag Singleton quickly slapped Seldon for weapons; with a man at each elbow, Seldon was ushered through the growing crowd and taken around the courthouse to the jail building. Fay came trailing after him; Seldon gave her a long, sharp glance and inclined his head in the direction of the Wagonwheel, but she refused to meet his eyes. When Munger and his men came shouldering into the cubbyhole office with their prisoner, Gary Strawn was with them, and so was Fay.

Easy Endicott was gone; he'd emptied desk drawers and stuffed the wastebasket, and he'd left his badge lying on the cleared desk top, but it was as though his personality still lingered in this office he'd occupied, some faint and intangible part of the just and tolerant law he'd represented. Then Munger reached for the badge, fastened it on his vest, and slumped into the swivel chair; and the illusion was lost.

Catching Strawn's eye, Seldon said, "You didn't waste much time getting a new sheriff."

Strawn shrugged. "Endicott turned in his resignation late this afternoon. When Munger came riding in a little later, I offered him the job. Singleton and Blue are deputies. That's all there is to it."

"I saw you ride in, Considine," Munger said. "Watched you from the window of Strawn's office in the courthouse. I should have shot you out of your saddle!"

Seldon understood then how Munger had come to be in Calumet ahead of him. Munger, having met up with Singleton after the affair at the riverbank cabin, had undoubtedly come to the cabin, discovered Ed Reeves's grave and noticed Seldon's and Fay's tracks headed toward town.

Munger, instead of trailing the two, must have taken a circuitous route to Calumet, riding hard, probably, and planning to be in town and waiting when his quarry arrived. But there was still much that Seldon didn't understand. "The county commissioners usually appoint a new sheriff to finish an unexpired term," he said, frowning. "And the chief deputy is the man in line for the job. What's the matter with Buck Prentiss? Did Limpy McSwain get him too?"

Strawn's voice turned brittle. "It happens the commissioners always left appointments to Judge Boaker. Since Boaker's gone, it was up to me to pick a new sheriff. Prentiss is a good man for taking orders, but he isn't sheriff-size. I don't know why the devil I have to explain my actions to you, Considine, but I wanted a sheriff who could think quick and shoot straight—a man to match Limpy McSwain in gun-savvy."

Anger put a high flush in Seldon's face. "So you picked an S-5 man while this basin's still sitting on the edge of a volcano that could erupt any day! What do you suppose the Raggedy Pants Pool's going to say to this?"

"I hadn't thought about it," Strawn countered.

"Then think about it now!" Seldon snapped. He reached into his pocket, a gesture that made the hands of Singleton and Blue move nervously, and he tossed Fenton's letter and map to the desk top. "There's the findings of the new survey," he said. "Look at them, Strawn. You'll see that both factions own separate stretches of the river. There's no need for a range war if Hurumpaw has lawmen who'll see that each side keeps to its own acres. And you picked Poe Munger for sheriff!"

Munger seized the map, spread it open, and had a look. "Here it is, Strawn," Munger said. "Just like I was telling you it would be. The old survey was right, and the upper Trinity is all on S-5 land. You gotta admit that gives us a legal right to build the dam I told you Banning was thinking about."

"The dam—!" Seldon ejaculated.

"Sure," Munger said, grinning. "Now that there's no question about the border line, we're free to go ahead and build a dam on the upper Trinity. That way S-5 can store water against a dry season. We couldn't make a move till now, but we'll be starting construction right away."

Seldon stiffened, seeing the whole scheme with startling clarity. "So you're bound to have a range war anyway!" he charged. "You'll build a dam that you don't need, just to cut off water from the lower river. You know confounded well the Raggedy Pants Pool will either have to fight you or get out!"

"Let 'em fight," Munger said. "They'll be on the wrong side of the fence, and we'll give 'em all the smoke they want. But you won't be hiring out your gun in that little fracas, mister. You're being jailed for killing Ed Reeves, and you're sitting in Limpy McSwain's old cell till you come to trial. I'm tired of listening to your jaw music. Take him away, boys."

Singleton and Blue each got hold of Seldon's elbows; he was shoved toward the door, and he discovered then that Fay had silently slipped away. He found a measure of relief in that fact; but before he was through the doorway, Munger said, "Just a minute, fellers. Yank that orange foofaraw off his throat. There's something I've been wanting to see for a long time."

Shag Singleton obliged, and with the neckerchief stripped away, Munger sucked in his breath, his squinted eyes narrowing. "No bullet scar from that wound that's supposed to give you your whispering voice," he observed. "I thought not. A helluva Hush Considine you are!"

Strawn quickened with interest. "Just *who* are you, mister? It might go easier if you told the truth."

Seldon smiled, a mere flashing of the teeth with no humor behind it. "I'm guessing that you've got your secrets, Strawn," he said. "I've got mine."

Singleton gave Seldon a shove, herding him down the

dim corridor and into the cell Limpy McSwain had occupied. The door clanged, a key grated, Singleton and Blue's boots went thumping off into silence, and Seldon stood gripping the door's bars for a long time. At last he turned to examine his cell, but there was little to see—a crude cot, a backless chair. The one window faced the gallows lot; its glass was in a hinged frame that had been swung inward; bars loomed dimly, for the darkness beyond was as yet unbroken on this cloud-obscured night. Seldon stepped toward the window, already hungry for the taste of fresh air, and that was when he heard a name whispered: "Considine!"

He came across the cell's narrow width in three strides, and he found a Bowie knife lying on the wooden sill that supported the window's bars. He called, "Fay!" softly, but there was no answer; boot soles slithered away in the gallows lot; and he stood holding the knife, his mind racing.

Freedom! He realized instantly to what good purpose this knife could be put. It would take a lot of hacking to get out of this log and frame structure through a wall, but the window's bars were set in a wooden framework, the point of the knife was sharp and strong, and diligent digging would remove those bars.

Yet suspicion held his hand. "Considine!" that unknown had called. Fay might have got the knife. Many men carried Bowies in sheaths at their belts. But Fay knew him to be Brad Seldon, not Hush Considine. Or had she called him by the assumed name from habit?

He didn't know. He held what might be a ticket to freedom or a passport to peril, depending on the intent of the person who'd left the knife. He thought of Limpy McSwain's empty grave and its weird portent; he thought of S-5's plan to build a dam on the upper Trinity and the trouble that would follow when the news reached the Raggedy Pants Pool. If he was to stop a range war, he had to be out of this cell, and that was the deciding factor for him. He began working with the knife, carefully chiseling at the base of one of the bars, his ears tuned for any sound in the corridor or the cubbyhole office beyond.

15 ⋮ Death Watch

Poe Munger stood waiting before the jail building, his stooped shoulders against the doorjamb, his fingers busy at fashioning a cigarette. Gary Strawn had crossed over to the courthouse; Singleton and Blue were off on special business; a dim lamp burned in the cell corridor, but the building was deserted, save for the prisoner. Cupping a match so that it spilled little light, a wary habit of long standing, Munger got his tobacco burning just as two figures loomed before him, men robbed of form and personality by the darkness until one of them spoke.

"He got the knife, Poe," Shag Singleton said. "And he's put 'er to work."

Munger inhaled smoke and satisfaction. "Think he saw you leave it?"

"Reckon not. He probably ain't too curious. Nobody looks a gift horse in the mouth."

Munger swore a Texas oath. "When you make a plan, take nothing for granted," he said. "Ed Reeves is coyote bait because he was maybe careless. Just let that sink into your skulls. Now we'd better get busy; there's work to do. Shag, go hunker yourself where you can keep an eye on that cell window. Blue, you start up this side of the street; I'll take the other. Drop in each saloon long enough for a drink, but don't lap up so much whisky you tangle your tongue. Make a little talk about a dam being built out on S-5; let it get around that we're going to work on it mighty quick—but not too quick. I don't want a flock of shovel stiffs out at the spread looking for jobs."

"I ain't sure I savvy—?" Blue began.

Munger made a gesture of irritation. "God, why is it a man can hire all the guns he wants, but there's never any brains attached to them? We're not really going to build a dam, savvy. Not unless the Pool figgers we're bluffing, and we have to start construction to convince 'em. But maybe talk will get 'em into a lather. There's probably a few Pool men in town; they'll hear what's said in the saloons. And they'll kill hosses carrying the news to Ord Wheeler."

"What about the Abbott girl?" Singleton asked. "She slipped out of the jail so quiet I never saw her go. But maybe she's still in town."

"Forget her," Munger decided after a moment's thoughtfulness. "I wanted her hogtied this morning so she couldn't carry word to Considine, or whatever his name is, but she doesn't matter now. Blue, when you've made the rounds of the saloons, come back here and join Shag. And be damn' sure the two of you don't bungle this! Wait till Considine's just about out of the jail before you start shooting. I want most of those bars removed, savvy, so we'll have proof to show if anybody doubts whether the prisoner was really trying to escape."

"You figger folks'll get wise that we turned lawmen to fry our own fish?" Singleton asked.

"Never mind the questions," Munger snapped. "Just do as I tell you—and do it right. I want Considine dead, understand."

He flicked his cigarette away and angled across the street, and Blue went sauntering down the opposite boardwalk. Watching them go, Singleton shrugged, then cat-footed into the gallows lot beside the jail. Moving cautiously, he found a place for himself behind the gallows platform; here he could see the jail window whenever he wished, yet he wouldn't be exposed if the moon showed itself. The night was rain-washed to a wholesome cleanness, but the air was chilly. Shivering, Singleton found the prospects of a long vigil not at all appealing.

Within fifteen minutes he was aching for a smoke, but he didn't dare risk a match so he resolutely put his mind against the need. Over yonder he could hear the faint scratching of Seldon's knife blade; down the street the saloons were noisy, the thousand sounds of the town blending into a discordant symphony. Time made its slow, relentless march, and finally Blue came crawling toward him, cautiously whispering his name.

"Fetched a short pint," Blue said, and produced a whisky bottle. "A man's got to keep the chill out of him. This much red-eye, split between us, won't shake our trigger fingers."

Singleton seized the bottle. "Hell, no," he said.

They drank, drawing their sleeves across their mouths, and Singleton asked, "Do yourself any good in the saloons?"

"Only saw one Pool man. He left in a hurry after I'd made my spiel. There'll be some tall cussin' across the Trinity afore sunup, I'm betting. How's Considine doing?"

Singleton edged around the platform for a look. The clouds were beginning to thin, the moon showed itself fleetingly, and Singleton grunted his disappointment at what the light revealed. "Ain't got the first bar out," he reported.

"Reminds me of Tucson," Blue said. "One night I watched a jigger clean up at poker, and I knew which trail he'd take. Seven hours I waited in the catclaw with lizards runnin' across my neck. Seven hours—"

The tale was long and rambling, and death was at its end. Singleton, stirred to memory, had an adventure from his own smoky past to match it, talking low-voiced and nipping at the bottle. Then, bored with each other, they fell silent.

"Where's Poe?" Singleton finally asked.

Blue shrugged. "Warming a chair, likely." He leaned for a look at the jail, and elation came into his voice. "Considine's got a bar out!"

"He packs a good pair o' shoulders," Singleton reflected. "He'll need at least three gone before he tries wigglin' through. Damn Poe for wanting to play this safe!"

Time dragged on, an hour and another hour; horsemen came along the street, men quitting the saloons to head for their varied destinations; boots hammered the boardwalks, the echoes fading into stillness; town lamps winked out, one by one, and a train made its melancholy lament in the distance.

"The westbound whistlin' for the Trinity bridge," Blue said needlessly.

"Considine's got another bar out," Singleton reported a moment later.

Still the death watch went on; the train came chuffing in at the depot far down the street; the shattered silence restored itself, and a wayfarer came up the boardwalk. His boots beat off into nothingness, and Blue said, "Wish I'd fetched another bottle. How's your hand?"

"Steady as a rock." Singleton got to his feet, peered around the gallows platform, then hastily backed away. "Third bar's out!" he husked. "He's trying to squeeze his shoulders through. And there's light for shooting!"

The moon was a ghostly horseman, pursued and harassed across the heavens but finding no lasting sanctuary in that writhing badlands of cloud wisps. Light glinted on gun barrels as Blue and Singleton both came to a stand, their long vigil ended, two men alike in looks and thought and purpose, brothers of the gun, merchants of death about to make delivery.

"He's gonna come out head first!" Singleton judged. "This'll be like shootin' fish in a rain-barrel. Who gets first try at him?"

"It'll only take one try," Blue said, and he edged his gun around the platform and sighted carefully. "Get yourself set, Shag. We'll take him at the same time. Hell, we're both deputy sheriffs, ain't we?"

* * *

Hard riding fetched Fay Abbott to the Wagonwheel at a record pace, but midnight was past when she turned her blown, lathered horse into the corral. She lurched a little as she crossed the rocky yard to the shack, and it seemed to her that she pounded upon the door for an interminable time before there was a stir inside. Then Ord Wheeler's voice came cautiously, saying, "Who's there?"

"Me—Fay! Let me in, Ord!"

The door opened; he stood there half-dressed and disheveled, sleep in his eyes and a six-gun dangling in his hand. Her excitement was all too evident; and as he let her into the room, he fumbled with a lamp and said, "What is it, Fay? What's up?"

"They've locked him in jail!" she cried. "They're framing a killing on him!" And then, because she suddenly realized that that carried no meaning to Wheeler, she made an effort to calm herself. "Considine, I mean," she explained. "Only he isn't Hush Considine. He's Brad Seldon, Cholla Sam's nephew."

Wheeler got an arm around her in his own awkward way. "You'd better tell it from the first," he said gently. "Take your time, Fay. Whatever's wrong can maybe be made right."

"It started this morning at S-5," she said and told of the talk she'd overheard between Munger and Banning, and of the chase and her meeting with Seldon, and the siege at the riverbank cabin. She spoke of Calumet and the empty grave, and the sheriff's badge Munger had got, and the S-5's plan to dam the upper Trinity. Wheeler heard her out in stunned silence, his dark brow wrinkling.

"So it's showdown now!" he said. "If they dam the river, we're finished. And if we fight 'em, we're finished, so long as Munger's toting a law badge. The dam must be the hole card Munger was talking about to Banning when you heard them!"

She said, "I don't care about the dam! Ord, don't you understand? It's Hush—Brad, I mean—I'm thinking of.

Whether they find out who he really is or not, they'll want him dead! You've got to save him!"

"Did you wire Cholla Sam?"

Her hands made a gesture of irritation. "A telegram wouldn't fetch him help for days! As soon as I slipped out of the jail, I rode here as fast as I could."

He said, "He's mighty important to you, isn't he?" He was a man seeing an obvious truth, yet flinching under its impact. "Just what's between you two, Fay?"

"He's in love with me," she said in a small voice.

"He told you that?"

"I knew for sure when he grew so terribly angry when I almost stopped a bullet in the cemetery. He showed I meant a lot to him. He kissed me afterward. And I'm in love with him, too, Ord. I guess I was from the first. I guess that's why I tried to keep telling myself that I hated him."

Some of the bluntness went out of Wheeler's jaw. "I never counted on anything like this," he said. "Never. And he's Cholla Sam's nephew. It might be better if he really was Hush Considine."

"But he's against Munger and Banning!" she cried. "He must be. He didn't have time for talking, but I can add two and two. Cholla Sam must have discovered something was wrong at S-5 and sent him to make it right. Probably he played Hush Considine so he could work undercover. Help him and you help yourself, Ord. I'm sure of it. He'll make a good neighbor out of the S-5."

Wheeler shook his head. "I wish I could be positive about that. I'm sorry for you, Fay, but I can see only one course for me. It's the Pool I've got to think about—the men who made me their boss because they figgered their fight would always be my fight. S-5's going to build a dam. That's what I'm thinking about. And that's what I've got to stop."

"He's in danger, Ord," she said, and she picked her words with cold and deliberate care. "I know he is, Ord; call it woman's intuition, if you wish. And if he dies without your lifting a hand to help him, I'll have to hate you as long as I live."

Her words turned him older, but after a while he said, "Do you think it's easy for me to think of the Pool ahead of you, Fay? It isn't. Believe me, if I thought he was in real danger, I'd saddle up and head to Calumet—for your sake. I owe you that much—and more. Don't worry. If a real showdown shapes for him, he'll tell who he is, and Gary Strawn will release him. Strawn might try prosecuting a wandering gunman like Hush Considine, just to build prestige, but Strawn's too smart a politician to buck the Seldons—especially since there's nothing in it for Strawn. Wait and see."

"He won't come to trial," she insisted. "He—"

Hoofs beat against the yard's rockiness, the Wagonwheel's dog began barking; Ord Wheeler grasped the gun he'd laid on a table, and was at the door in a single bound, but the tension went out of his wide shoulders as he saw the man who was dismounting. He was a stooped, gray-whiskered homesteader whose place was south of Cowper's Ford; his name was Onsum, and he'd half killed a horse getting here.

"Come in," Wheeler said.

"Glad you're up," Onsum panted. "I just come from town. Poe Munger was making talk in the Staghorn tonight. Said S-5 had claim to all the upper Trinity on account of the new survey and—"

"I know—they're going to build a dam," Wheeler said, gesturing toward Fay.

Onsum doffed his sombrero; like all the other homesteaders, he knew there was some relationship between Wheeler and this girl, but he'd never been sure what it was. Months ago Wheeler and Fay had decided the truth should be kept secret as long as Fay worked for S-5. Onsum said, "It looks like we're licked for good."

"Unless we fight," Wheeler said.

Fay looked at Wheeler. "Then you won't wait till Seldon has a chance to show what he intends to do?"

Wheeler said, "I'll do this much for you, Fay—I'll wait till Seldon shows his hand. But meanwhile I'm going to gather the Pool and have the boys ready for war. Onsum, will you take one of my saddlers and do some riding? Head south along the Trinity and send every homesteader up here to the Wagonwheel. Don't waste any time at it, though. Your job is to cut sign on Easy Endicott and fetch him back here. We've got to talk him into taking his badge again. We'll have some chance with him as a lawman—none with Munger. Now you'd better get started. I'll collect the boys to the north of here."

The talk between Wheeler and Fay had put questions in Onsum's eyes, but he was a man who could appreciate time's worth when a crisis shaped, so he clapped on his sombrero and strode to the door. "I'll send the men along," he promised. "With guns."

When he'd gone, astride a borrowed saddler, Wheeler finished his dressing, Fay watching him silently. As he buckled on his gun-belt, she said, "You just won't go to Calumet, is that it?"

"I've got to get the Pool together and ready," he insisted. "Think, Fay! Munger's got a badge now; suppose he deputized all his S-5 gunnies and brought them across the Trinity on some pretext. I told you I'd wait till young Seldon shows his hand. But meanwhile I've got to be ready."

Fresh arguments, new pleas, thronged through her head; but she left them unspoken, for she was beginning to see Wheeler's position. There was much stubbornness in this big-bodied brother of hers; he lacked her deeper perception, her quick way of thinking, but he did a job as he saw it. And suddenly she remembered a thousand hardships they'd shared, the things that bound them more than the blood; and the realization came to her of what a home meant and why he must fight for his, if needs be. "Good luck, Ord," she said. "Maybe it's only that I love him so much that I'm afraid."

He smiled. "He'll come back to you soon. Please wait here, Fay. I don't want to have to worry about you, too."

She nodded, and that made it a promise; but when he'd gone, she fell to pacing, fighting against her growing fears, trying desperately to reassure herself. Once she fingered the letter from Texas that Seldon had given her, and she wondered if she should open it but decided to wait. The cot Wheeler had deserted stood in the corner, disordered but inviting, and at last she stretched upon it, telling herself she'd only rest for a moment. But sleep overtook her, a troubled sleep threaded with strange, incoherent dreams; and she awoke when hoofs rattled in the yard again, awoke to find the dawn etching the windows a pearly gray.

Ord had come back, and with him were half a dozen homesteaders who lived to the north. Rubbing the sleep from her eyes, Fay stirred up a fire in the cooking range as they unsaddled. Soon they came trooping in, and she made them breakfast and watched them eat it, studying their silent restraint and knowing that these were men acutely aware that they faced a fight.

By midmorning other Pool men came drifting in, small ranchers from the south who'd been sent by Onsum; and they filled the shack to overflowing and spilled out into the yard, where they gathered in tight little groups. Fay remembered another day when they'd left their women and children behind—the day when the Raggedy Pants Pool had ridden into Calumet to stop a hanging.

She quizzed many of them about town, hoping there'd be news of Seldon; but no man among them had been in Calumet today. More came with the passing hours; and at last Onsum himself put in an appearance, riding another borrowed saddler, and his face was long and grave.

"You didn't find Endicott?" Wheeler guessed.

"I found him," Onsum reported. "He got as far away

from Calumet as the railroad bridge. I found him hanging from one of the supports by his neck, his hands tied behind him. He'd been knocked on the head beforehand, I'd judge. Limpy McSwain can tally another one. I cut Endicott down and heaped rocks on him to keep the coyotes away, but somebody'll have to do a decent buryin' job when there's more time to spare."

Fay heard the murmur go up from the gathered men, the desolated murmur of a hope blasted beyond repair. Another time the news might have shocked and angered her; she'd known Easy Endicott and liked him. But she was drained of all emotion save anxiety; her heart was in Calumet, her heart called for news from Calumet, and there was none to bring her news.

Shortly after that she quietly saddled her horse and rode away from the Wagonwheel. She'd kept her promise to Wheeler by awaiting his return. Some saw her leave, but Ord was busy in the shack, and no one challenged her. She headed down the river toward Cowper's Ford, intending to go to Calumet but not knowing what she'd do when she got there.

She had to find out what had become of Brad Seldon, and she rode along oblivious to all else but that insistent thought, and she came to the ford near noon and made the crossing and headed her mount through the fringing willows and up the first rise. And there, in the shadow of that rocky buttress of thronging memories, she found the man who sat his saddle, blocking her trail.

16 ⋮ That Letter From Texas

To Brad Seldon, working away at the cell window, the night had been interminably long. Like Singleton and Blue, Seldon heard the blatant roar of the saloons, the plop of hoofs, the beating boots along the boardwalk, and the train's whistling. These were the sands of an exceedingly noisy hourglass; he measured the hours by interpreting these various sounds, and several times he'd been almost certain that he heard low-voiced talk over yonder where the gallows stood in spidery silhouette.

He couldn't be sure. Stopping his chiseling time and again to listen intently, his suspicion remained only a suspicion, so he'd resumed work. The first bar removed, he'd set it into its socket again, surveying his work with a certain pride, satisfied that nothing would look amiss to anyone coming along the corridor. Then he'd put the bar on the floor to give himself more elbow room as he tackled the next bar.

He had the second bar removed when the train whistled for the Trinity bridge, and the third bar proved easiest of all. When he lifted it out, he experimentally squeezed his shoulders through the opening; by tight squirming he could make his escape without removing the fourth and last bar, he discovered. And then the outer door of the jail banged open, and boots came slogging along the cell corridor.

Turning hastily away from the window, Seldon's disappointment was as acute as physical pain. No time now to put those bars back in place; the men who were coming down the corridor were already at the cell door. They'd see his handiwork, and they'd remove him to another cell and watch him closely thereafter. Sliding the Bowie into his boot top, Seldon stood with his back to the window as Gary Strawn, jangling a key ring, fumbled at the door. Poe Munger was with him, standing back a pace, his hard mouth pulled down petulantly at the corners. But it was the third man who chained Seldon's eyes—the big-bodied, frock-coated man with the unlighted cigar in his mouth.

"Howdy, Judge!" Seldon cried and strode joyfully across the cell's narrow width. "You're the heftiest *habeas corpus* I ever saw! When did you get back?"

"Tonight's train," Boaker said. In the corridor's uncertain light, he looked wan and ghastly, his healthy pink replaced by an ashy grayness. "Heard a little talk down at the depot about the excitement in town tonight, and I came right up here. Gary had a light burning in his office; otherwise you might have had to sit until morning. Sorry the law made a mistake about you, boy."

Munger said, "I'm still wondering if it *was* a mistake. Take a look at the window, Judge. He was bustin' himself out; can't you see it? If he's so all-fired innocent as you think, what was the idea?"

But Boaker gave him no answer, and Strawn, opening the door, said, "Come out, Seldon. Why in blazes didn't you tell me who you were in the first place?"

"That was my ace-in-the-hole, Strawn. It suited me to keep it till the last hand was dealt. But maybe that time is here."

They came up into the cubbyhole office, Strawn gnawing at his mustache. "I hope you'll understand my attitude, Seldon," he said. "When Munger brought a charge against you, I had to consider the reputation of Hush Considine, which isn't any too savory. Once Boaker told me you were Cholla Sam's nephew, that put a different complexion on the matter. If you shot Ed Reeves, I presume you had a good reason."

"Don't let it work you into a lather, old son," Seldon said and glanced at Boaker. "Are you letting Munger keep the sheriff's badge, Judge?"

"Of course not!" Boaker snapped. "Strawn, it looks like I came back at just about the right time. I'm not accusing you of anything but thoughtlessness, though you seem to have been mighty long on that. Munger—of all men!"

"But Limpy McSwain—" Strawn began.

"To the devil with Limpy McSwain! We've got more than him to worry about. Buck Prentiss is taking Endicott's place, understand. Buck's got as much reason to hunt down McSwain as anybody, if that's what you want, but Buck hasn't any private irons in the fire. Munger, get that badge off you! I'll have no man in this office who's definitely lined up with one faction or another."

Strawn said, "Probably you're right, Judge. I've admitted I made a mistake about Seldon here, but aren't you taking sides when you insist he be set free? The Pool will hear about this, and they're bound to learn who he really is. What will *they* think?"

"They'll think I did justice—if they stop to use their heads," Boaker countered. "Strawn, can't you get this straight? The law of Hurumpaw isn't playing politics, and it isn't lining up with S-5 or the Pool, either. If I'd come home to find Ord Wheeler in jail on such a flimsy charge, I'd have had you rattling your keys just as fast. Now go and find Buck Prentiss and tell him he's got a sheriffing job to do."

Words writhed on Strawn's lips, but he left them unspoken. He stood stiffly, his eyes meeting Boaker's; and Seldon, watching, remembered that once he'd judged these two men and decided that the real strength lay in Gary Strawn. Seldon wasn't so sure now; he knew that Strawn could still be a hard man to cross, but the lawyer meekly said, "All right, Judge. See you in the morning."

Strawn started for the door; and Munger, who'd silently unpinned his badge and tossed it onto the desk, trailed along. But Seldon said, "Just a minute, Munger. You'll probably go on record as the man who lost two jobs in five minutes' time. I came here on the q.t. to sort the grays from the blacks, and I've got you pegged proper. You're fired from S-5; you can find Singleton and Blue and tell them the same thing goes for them. I'll take personal pleasure in handing out walking papers to the rest of your gun-handy crew myself."

Munger peeled back his lips. "Bucko, you're riding high—now!" he snapped. "The last hand hasn't been played yet."

"You'd better not be around when it is," Seldon said. "If you're not headed out of the basin by sunup, I'll tell the sheriff—the *new* sheriff—what happened at the Hurumpaw water tank. Now git!"

Munger went, his boots clumping angrily along the boardwalk; Seldon rummaged in the desk and found his own gun, then turned to Boaker with a wan smile. "I'm obliged, Judge," he said. "I reckon you're tired and anxious for bed. I'll walk to your cottage with you."

Boaker blew out the lamp and took the key for the outer door. "Come along," he said. "I want to know everything that's happened while I was in Helena."

Outside, they started up the street, but abreast of the gallows lot Seldon said, "Just a minute." Walking toward the gallows, he cupped a match and had a look around, seeing an empty whisky bottle and the marks of bootheels where two men had hunkered, waiting. Nothing more. Rejoining the judge, they went on toward the cottage; and in the shadow of the veranda they loitered, Seldon talking and Boaker listening; and when Seldon ran out of words, most of the night was gone.

"I'll be heading to S-5," Seldon said then. "I've got to fire the crew, and I'm having a showdown with Banning. If he's authorized the building of a dam, he's overstepped himself. Likewise he's proved he wants a range war, even if he has to buy one. I'm still not sure about him, but I'm through with waiting. But first I've got to see Fay Abbott. She's got that letter I told you about."

Boaker yawned. "We should have gone inside and been comfortable," he observed. "But you'll want to be on your way, son. Good luck to you."

Seldon took the judge's proffered hand. "Do you own a gun, amigo?" he asked. "Oh, you still have the one you borrowed from Endicott the morning McSwain was hanged. Good! Sleep with it handy, feller. I don't want anything happening to you."

He went back up the street, feeling weary but far too excited to seek rest. His horse, left at the jail's hitchrack long hours ago, had been gone, he'd noticed; but Munger, as sheriff, had probably put the roan in the livery stable. Rousing the hostler, Seldon found that his guess had been right. Ten minutes later he was heading out of Calumet in the direction of Cowper's Ford, and somewhere in the tangled terrain between the town and the crossing he met Buck Prentiss riding toward him.

"Howdy," Seldon said when they'd both reined up. "I take it you haven't seen Strawn."

The squat little deputy fumbled for the makings, built himself a cigarette, and passed the tobacco to Seldon. "I took a pasear," Prentiss said. "Right after Sid was cut down and Easy opened Limpy's grave and decided sheriffing wasn't a healthy job. Thought I might cut a little sign."

"On Limpy? Any luck?"

Prentiss shook his head. "That Limpy McSwain makes one helluva angel. Yet he's sprouted himself a pair of wings since we hung him. But there's some excitement stirring across the Trinity. Met up with a homesteader named Onsum who was out playin' Paul Revere. They're gathering for war because S-5's talking about building a dam on the upper river."

"That dam won't be built," Seldon said emphatically. "Buck, Judge Boaker came home last night. He's making you sheriff; he'll tell you all about it when you get to town."

He thrust out his hand. "I'm Brad Seldon, Buck—nephew to old Cholla Sam. I had my reasons for playing it different."

Prentiss shook hands. "Figgered you weren't what you seemed to be," he said laconically. "Can you stop this war?"

"I'm going to try," Seldon promised. "Be seeing you."

He jogged his horse onward, feeling better for this brief meeting with Hurumpaw's new sheriff, but growing impatient to be at his destination. The dawn broke around him; he came to Cowper's Ford in late morning, pausing in the shadow of the rocky buttress that topped the first rise, and here he could see the placid crossing and the rider who was using the ford; and he sat his saddle, drinking in the sight of her, until she was almost to him.

"Hello, Fay," he said.

After last night in the cemetery, he would always look upon her with new eyes; the memory of their kiss still burned, but all that had been under the stress of danger, and he felt not at all sure of himself now. Women had played their small part in his life, but he laid no claim to a knowledge of them. Fay said, "Oh!" and went limp in her saddle; and then she had righted herself and was smiling, and the moment was lost when he might have had the courage to take her in his arms.

"Judge Boaker came to town and played my ace-in-the-hole for me," he explained. "Strawn turned me loose once he discovered who I was. I was coming to the Wagonwheel, Fay."

She said, "Ord claimed it would be that way once Strawn knew the truth. Brad, I'm so glad to see you!"

Flippancy had served him in the past, and he wondered why he should be so self-conscious now. To cover his confusion, he said, "You've still got that letter from Texas?"

She passed it over. "Brad, the Pool's gathering for war, but unless S-5 makes trouble meanwhile, Ord's agreed to wait till you show your hand. And Easy Endicott's dead, Brad. One of the homesteaders found him hanging from the railway trestle. It's bad—bad!"

His lips tightening at this news, he ran his thumb under the flap of the envelope and shook out the sheets covered with the familiar scrawl of his Ranger captain. His glance made apology to Fay; and he began reading, his interest growing as his eyes shuttled back and forth along the lines. When he'd finished, he sat holding the letter, lost in reverie until Fay's voice recalled him.

"Hadn't we better be getting to the Wagonwheel?"

"No," he said slowly. "I'm going to S-5. Come along, if you wish; it should be safe enough. Poe Munger's left this range, I reckon, and I'll only have one man to handle —the man I've got to see. Fay, if I'd had this letter in my pocket the day I rode into the basin, I'd have settled all this affair pronto. I'm thinking it's good news we'll fetch Ord Wheeler before sundown."

She showed her puzzlement. "This man—?" she asked. "Do you mean Banning?"

"You know him by one name—Texas by another," he said grimly. "My business is with the only man on S-5 who answers to the law's old description of the Lampassa Kid."

17 ⋮ Rider at Moonrise

They looked upon S-5's sprawling buildings from the crest of a bluff, seeing little sign of life. Smoke curled from the chimney of the cook-shack where Ki wrought his magic; the golden collie, Shep, dozed before the ranch-house doorway; a few saddlers stomped in the corrals, but the crew was not in evidence. Studying all this, Seldon said, "Seems safe enough, Fay. Yet the crew's being gone worries me. Where do you suppose they went?"

Fay shook her head. "Maybe Banning's with them."

"We'll see," he said and nudged his horse.

As they stepped down from saddles before the ranch-yard gate, Shep, stirring to life, came joyously to Fay, barking and bounding; and thus they were innocently betrayed, for Banning's face was a smear at his office window, and then he was gone. Seldon ran quickly to the door, not knocking this time but thrusting inward and lunging along the hall. Banning stood framed in the doorway giving out of his office. He said, "Considine! What the devil are you doing here?"

Seldon smiled. "I've got two days' wages coming. I might be here to collect, but I'm not. It's time for a facing of the cards, Banning. I'm Brad Seldon."

Banning backed into his office, Seldon moving after him and Fay following close behind. Banning said thickly, "What sort of nonsense is this?" But he crossed to that framed photograph on the wall, the picture of a roundup crew, and he studied the high-boned features of a younger

Cholla Sam, then swung around for a thoughtful appraisal of Brad Seldon.

"By God, maybe you *are* a Seldon!" Banning said. "Why didn't you tell me in the first place, man?"

Seldon ignored the question. "Where's your crew?"

Banning shrugged. "Munger sent them somewhere yesterday; they've been gone since."

"I see," Seldon said. "Now tell me this, Banning. When Cholla Sam hired you, did he know you were an escaped convict from the Texas penitentiary by the name of the Lampassa Kid?"

Banning had mastered his first surprise at learning Seldon's identity; now he reeled as though struck by a fist, the bigness of him going limp. He leaned against his desk, fighting for speech. At last he said, "That means I'm finished here—"

Seldon shrugged. "Cholla Sam sent me to right whatever was wrong at S-5. I took my time because I had to be sure. You haven't been working for him, Banning. You've sided a bunch of crooks in a scheme they've almost put over—thanks to your help. Yes, you're finished, Banning. What else could you expect?"

Banning said, "I don't know how much you've learned, or how you found it out. But will you hear my side of it? Even if it's the pen for me again, I'd like Cholla Sam to know the truth."

Fay's eyes were on Seldon, making a mute appeal. Folding his arms, Seldon said, "I'm listening, Banning."

"I'm Lampassa all right," Banning admitted. "I rode long spurs, and I made a name for myself in Texas, and it's nothing to be proud of now. Train-robbing—rustling—I tried everything. That was twenty-two years ago; I was eighteen then, and many an older man was in the pack that rode with me."

"Poe Munger for one," Seldon interjected. "And Shag Singleton and Blue and Ed Reeves and Limpy McSwain, and that other fellow, probably—the one I knocked off the jail roof. I've seen a list of the names, Banning. You had quite a crew."

Banning gazed at the floor. "But I tripped up finally and went to trial. I had one of the best lawyers in Texas, but he couldn't keep me out of the pen. They took me through those big gates, and I was laughing; I was the Lampassa Kid, and I'd give any warden gray hairs who tried taming me! But I lived to learn. No, there wasn't a whip used, or anything like that. They put me in solitary, buried me alive in a dirty, crawling dungeon. They cut me off from the sunshine and left me to think it over, days on end, only all of them were nights." His voice broke, the forgotten horror creeping into his eyes. "They broke me all right; they had me begging to be put on a rock pile."

"And then you escaped? How was that worked, Banning? I'd guess that you had outside help. Your old gang?"

Banning nodded. "They had horses ready, and they fixed everything, but somebody else did their thinking for them. No, he wasn't a friend of mine. There was something he wanted. You see, I'd hidden away loot on my lonesome before I was captured—loot that added up to plenty. That's why they sprung me from prison; it was more money than the bunch had seen in a long time. They hadn't found pickings easy with the Lampassa Kid in stony lonesome."

"You'd served three years," Seldon said. "You still owed the State of Texas a lot of time. But you got away, and that was just about the last ever heard of the Lampassa Kid. Your old bunch must have done a good job of covering your sign."

Banning said, "I slipped away from them the very first night I was free. You've got to believe that, Seldon, and you've got to make Cholla Sam believe it. The Lampassa Kid was dead as far as I was concerned, understand! The Lampassa Kid got put in prison and had the spirit taken out of him; I never wanted a taste of that again. I rode north alone, and I wrote the warden from Kansas and told him where he'd find all the loot I'd left buried."

Seldon smiled. "I'll bet Munger and the others liked *that!*"

"I drifted into Montana, finally," Banning went on. "I got a job at S-1, and I worked hard and studied hard. I learned cattle and ranching, but I schooled myself from books, too. I wanted to change personalities, to stamp out the last trace of the old Lampassa Kid, and I must have succeeded. For Cholla Sam finally offered me the management of S-5."

"But you never told him the whole truth."

"I tried! I told him there was something about my past he ought to know. He cussed me out—said it didn't matter what a man had been; he was only interested in what I was. Do you think, Seldon, that it was easy to double-cross a man like Cholla Sam?"

"I'm beginning to understand," Seldon murmured. "Your old friends tracked you here, I suppose?"

"The first one came not long after; he settled here but never gave any sign that he knew me. For a while I breathed easy, thinking perhaps I'd changed so much that he wasn't sure. But I was living in a fool's paradise, those first years. Then Munger came."

"And you had to hire him?"

"He rode up and asked for a job. When I refused him, he laid a newspaper clipping on my desk—an account of the arrest of the Lampassa Kid. It's locked in yonder safe. He said the other one had located him and sent for him, that first man who'd come, and he threatened to tip off Texas law about me if I didn't string along. That was when I learned about the big scheme they had."

"To rule Hurumpaw?"

Banning nodded. "That was the idea. Munger packed the crew with gunhands, stirred up trouble with the homesteaders, making sure he didn't overstep and arouse the law's suspicion. The whole scheme hinged on starting a range war. That way we'd drive the Pool out of the basin and ruin S-5 at the same time. Cholla Sam, with ranches scattered all over, has a reputation to consider, and with big trouble here and S-5 in the red, he'd be willing to sell at a dime on the dollar. The kingpin of our bunch figured on buying then. The rest of us would take the Pool's deserted homesteads, and we'd have the whole basin in our hands."

Seldon shook his head. "The whole deal's been played to perfection," he said. "What chance did Ord Wheeler have when the very men he hired, McSwain and those others, were really on your side? And Cholla Sam was trusting you all the while you were systematically ruining S-5. You should be mighty proud of yourself, Banning!"

"You're entitled to your scorn," Banning said. "I know I've no backbone. Even Munger noticed that, but it's the thought of prison that's kept me hogtied. But this is the part you've got to get straight, Seldon. I'm still beholden to Cholla Sam. I've hated every move they've forced me to make. Maybe, when the real showdown came, I might have been true to my salt. I don't know. And I've lost the chance to ever find out."

He glanced at Fay. "The night Boaker was hanged, you accused me of masquerading as Limpy McSwain. I told you then that I had every reason for wanting Boaker alive. And I did. So long as his kind of law held sway in the Hurumpaw, the big scheme was going to be hard to put over."

"What about McSwain?" Seldon interjected. "Is he alive?"

"I don't know. Munger doesn't know, either. McSwain, or whoever's pretending to be McSwain, is playing a lone-wolf game."

Seldon crossed to the office window. Outside the sunshine spread itself lavishly, peace brooded upon the place, bees droned in the flowers fringing the house; and Shep was rounding a corner, padding off toward the barn on some silent expedition. But Seldon saw none of this; his mind had gone back across the years—back to the time a wild youngster had ridden under the Texas moon, a youngster called the Lampassa Kid. Quick of imagination, Seldon could understand how it had been with the Lampassa Kid, and he could feel the horror of those endless days in that stony city without a soul, the penitentiary. He turned then—turned to face a man who had sinned and repented and, in his own weak way, sinned again. Fay had crossed to Banning; her hand was on Banning's arm, and she said, "I'm sorry, Gus. Very sorry."

"And I'm sorry for you too, Banning," Seldon said. "You see, no man was ever so thoroughly double-crossed as you. It's obvious there's something you don't know. When you wrote from Kansas, telling where your loot was hidden, restitution was made to a lot of people, and the governor reconsidered your case. A wise, kindly man, he knew the difference between a badman and a hot-blooded kid with adventure in him. He issued you a full pardon, Lampassa."

Banning stared blankly. *"A pardon!"*

Seldon nodded. "Of course you'd have to go back to Texas to straighten out certain technicalities. But the pardon was issued years ago, just the same. It was turned over to your lawyer, that same lawyer who defended you, a man who is a disgrace to an old and honorable profession. He never told you about the pardon, did he? You haven't mentioned his name yet, Banning, but I know him. I'm meaning the kingpin—the man who first tracked you here, saw his chance to grab off a range empire, and sent for Munger and the others. I'm meaning the man who's used you as his tool—Gary Strawn."

Fay gasped. "So that's why he came here so often! And you rode into town to see him the night Boaker was attacked, Gus!"

"I've suspected Strawn ever since the night that Munger knew exactly what train Charlie Fenton would be on," Seldon said. "Boaker sent for Fenton, but Strawn handled the correspondence."

Banning shook his head, saying numbly over and over again, "A pardon—a pardon—"

"Strawn had a club against you, and he wasn't throwing it away," Seldon went on relentlessly. "But I got the story from my Ranger captain, who checked old records for me. That newspaper clipping is gone from the safe, Banning. Fay took it, along with the survey field notes. She's Ord Wheeler's half sister, which means she's favored the Pool. But I'll say this for her; she's the one person on S-5 who's really been working for Cholla Sam Seldon."

Banning raised his stricken eyes. "That clipping mentioned that Strawn was defending me. It was in the last paragraph. He saw the clipping here one day, tore off the end and told me I'd better keep the clipping out of sight."

"Too bad," Seldon said. "If I'd seen the whole account, I might have put things together without writing to Texas."

From the doorway, Poe Munger said, "Hoist 'em, Seldon!" He stood there in his stockinged feet, a gun level in his hand, Shag Singleton crowding behind him. "You made the mistake of leaving your horse standing in plain sight at the gate, Seldon," Munger went on. "It was the same as a calling-card. I told you the last hand hadn't been played yet. Your luck's run out."

He came padding into the office, Singleton after him, and Banning stood staring blankly, showing no elation at this unexpected rescue. Munger gave him a sharp glance and said, "What's eating *you?*"

Banning said, "Texas issued a pardon to me, Poe. Strawn got it—and Strawn kept it."

Munger laughed. "I knew that," he said. "What about it?"

"You knew!" Banning cried, and suddenly he came lunging across the room at Munger, charging with his arms outstretched and his eyes wild. Singleton took a sideward step, swung his gun barrel in a short, chopping blow that caught Banning across the scalp, and S-5's manager went to his knees, still conscious but with the fight beaten out of him.

Munger glanced at him, no show of emotion in the foreman's face. "I had a hunch it would come to this sometime," he said.

Singleton, the smell of blood in his nostrils, swung his gun barrel toward Seldon. "There's a slug I didn't get to use last night!" Singleton said flatly. "Now, damn you—!"

"Shag!" Munger's bark was like the snapping of a whip. "Not now! We're keeping him alive for a while. He's Cholla Sam's nephew, you fool! He'll make a good hostage when we dicker with Cholla Sam to take over S-5 at our own price. Collect their guns, then fetch a rope and tie their hands, all three of them."

Singleton scowled, but he obeyed, tossing the guns into a corner, then leaving to return with a rope which he hacked into short lengths with which he methodically bound the hands of the three behind their backs. Banning was more alive now, but he held his tongue; and Seldon and Fay kept silent, too. Munger considered the trio thoughtfully, then said, "That old harness room in the barn ought to hold them."

Singleton said, "Supposing Ki finds 'em there?"

"He won't. I'll send him to town for a load of grub."

The prisoners were prodded to the porch; here Munger pulled on the boots he'd discarded for the sake of silence, and Blue came riding up then, swinging from his saddle and stalking into the yard. He eyed the prisoners with some surprise.

"Just got back from the river, boss," he reported to Munger. "The boys are strung out between the island and Cowper's Ford. Something's stirrin' across the Trinity, that's sure, but the Pool hasn't made a real move yet."

Seldon stiffened with interest, sensing a trap waiting to be sprung, and he broke his silence then. "You're overstepping this time, Munger. You see, the Pool knows who I am, and they won't cross the river till they find out how I stand. Carry your war over to the Pool, and you'll have the law against you. Boaker's back, remember, and Prentiss is sheriff, and Strawn will have to play dead dog."

Munger turned angry eyes on Banning. "How much did you tell him, you fool!" He gnawed at his lip for a long and thoughtful moment, and then his eyes lighted. "We can't keep waiting forever," he said. "Blue, head back to the river and take two, three boys out to that little island. Light a fire and get it smoking. That will fetch Wheeler; it's a signal him and this girl use. When he comes, get him— but get him alive. He may make a good hostage, too. I'm gambling he'll come alone, figgering the girl's got news for him only. And I'm bettin' the Pool will cross the Trinity when Wheeler doesn't show back."

Fay said, "You dirty, scheming devil—!"

Munger slapped her hard across the mouth, and Singleton's prodding gun barrel stopped Seldon's wild lunge. Blue walked toward his horse; Munger and Singleton herded their prisoners from the porch and around the corner toward the barn. Inside the shadowy spaciousness of the big building, they were propelled past the stalls and into a little, box-like room lighted by one small window, a room with harness hanging from pegs and odds and ends littering the floor. Here Singleton forced the three to lie down; their ankles were trussed, the door closed behind them, and they were alone.

Seldon said, "I never counted on Munger staying in the basin. I thought I had the game busted; I should have known that being backed against the wall would only make men like Strawn and Munger desperate. God, if I could only get out of here!"

He fell to struggling with the rope at his wrist, but the knots defied him. He worked with feverish frenzy, and Fay and Banning also tried freeing themselves. It was stifling hot in this little room; sweat broke over Seldon, running into his eyes and blinding him, making his clothes a torture.

At last he gave up the effort, lying quietly and promising himself he'd gather new strength. But the sleepless hours of last night exacted their toll; he drifted off into slumber in spite of himself, awaking as boots thudded along the barn's board floor hours later. The door opened; Ord Wheeler, hatless and disheveled, was shoved inside by Blue, and the Pool leader was tripped to the floor and his ankles were trussed.

"Who's here?" Wheeler demanded when Blue had gone. Twilight had come and the harness room's interior was a pocket of dusk.

Seldon told him. "You fell for their ruse," he added bitterly. "But it was too much to hope that you wouldn't." He spoke at length of Munger's plan, told Wheeler the truth about Strawn and Banning, and the Pool leader heard him out, cursing softly.

"So now the cards are faced," Wheeler said. "And a lot of good it does!" He writhed for a moment, straining at his ropes. "If I only had a knife!"

"*A knife!*" Seldon echoed. "There's one in my boot top—a present from some friends," he added grimly. "I'd forgotten I'd put it there, and I know Singleton didn't find it when he tied my ankles. He was too blind from coming out of sunlight. Wheeler, wiggle over this way. See if you can get your fingers on it!"

Wheeler came inching across the floor. Getting to a sitting position, he maneuvered himself to put his back to Seldon's feet, and a few moments later Wheeler grunted triumphantly. The knife in his hands, he and Seldon changed positions, putting themselves back to back while Wheeler tried hacking at Seldon's bonds.

It was slow, awkward work. Wheeler's wrists were bound too tightly to give him any real freedom of movement, and time and again Seldon felt the steel's sharpness against his skin. The blood came; but he made no complaint, urging Wheeler to greater effort.

"Try pulling on the rope!" Wheeler panted at last. "I think I got it partly sawed through."

Seldon strained with effort. "No good," he reported.

"Listen!" Fay suddenly cried. "Hoofbeats! Somebody's riding up to the barn!"

They all fell silent, trying hard to hear. Out in the yard, Shep was growling a deep-voiced threat, punctuated by sharp, angry barks; and then a gun spoke, the report flat and remote, and Shep's growling ceased.

"He's killed Shep!" Fay cried, her voice trailing away as someone came walking into the barn, walking with a peculiar shuffling limp. The footsteps ceased; outside the harness room a man fumbled, and the door creaked open. Night had settled, but the one window faced east and the first light of the rising moon touched the intruder as he stood framed in the opened doorway. A high-shouldered man, his face was still in shadow, but Seldon saw that he wore a faded blue shirt and levis glazed with dirt. And over one arm he carried a coiled lariat, its end a hangman's noose dangling in his hand.

The four lay watching him in hypnotized silence; his eyes flitted from one to another until his gaze lingered on Seldon. And to Seldon this moment was like the one at the foot of the gallows that day Limpy McSwain had looked at him in like fashion and threatened death to all Hurumpaw lawmen and to Seldon as well.

18 ⋮ Guns Along the Trinity

To Seldon this was like a nightmare that persisted beyond the waking point, a fantasy, utterly unbelievable, that was at the same time actuality. He'd heard the tales of a dead man riding; he'd seen Limpy McSwain's empty grave, but looking upon Hurumpaw's phantom hangman was different. A man detached from himself, Seldon watched the intruder come into the harness room, saw the man's eyes rove to the rafters above. The rope the fellow carried was shaken out and sent spinning over a hook bolted into one of the rafters, a hook from which a saddle might have hung.

Still Seldon could only stare in fascinated silence. He knew this man was here to hang him; perhaps to hang the others as well. He knew it was only a matter of minutes until that noose was adjusted around his neck, and he was hauled to a writhing, strangling death. Yet the reality of it left him untouched.

Then the man reached and got a grasp on Seldon, hauling him to an awkward stand, an effort revealing an amazing strength for a man so lanky of build. Fay screamed, the sound trailing off to an eerie sob; Wheeler cursed steadily and monotonously as the noose was settled about Seldon's neck; Banning sucked in his breath sharply. But Seldon was no longer a man caught in a sluggish nightmare; the touch of the intruder had broken the trance. Seldon stood now with a full awareness of his danger, a man about to die and made desperate by that fact. He strained at the rope binding his wrists, strained with a new and frantic strength. And suddenly the rope, weakened by Wheeler's knife-work, parted, and Seldon's hands were free.

Slowed circulation had made his arms wooden, but he sent his left fist forward in a blind blow at the shadowy figure before him, his knuckles smashing against the man's chest, his arm tingling to the shoulder. But that was like wielding a paper club; so Seldon bent his head and butted hard, trying to catch the intruder in the midriff; but Seldon's ankles were still bound, and he went off balance, sprawling headlong. He shouted, "Banning! Wheeler! Grab him!"

It wasn't a ruse; his mind was still too muddled for clear thinking; it was a cry wrung out of desperation, but it had its effect. The intruder obviously hadn't expected to find a man able to fight. Taken by surprise, the fellow lunged for the door and got through it and beyond, his boots thudding the length of the barn.

His fingers all thumbs, Seldon fumbled at the knots binding his ankles, cursing his numbness. And then, remembering, he felt along the floor for the knife Wheeler had been using. Getting hold of it, he slashed at the rope, freeing himself, and he lurched toward the harness room door, his step unsteady.

"Let him go, Brad!" Fay cried. "He'll kill you!"

But Seldon was far too angry to measure consequences. He went charging through the barn, his growing rage giving him an urgent desire to get his hands on the phantom hangman; and he lurched out into the yard to see the fellow swinging into a saddle a hundred yards away. Seldon shouted incoherently, still running forward; the man twisted in his kak, a gun in his hand, and laid a shot in Seldon's direction. Sprawling, Seldon flattened himself against the ground, fearful of a second shot, knowing what an easy target he made, and wishing mightily for a gun. But the rider didn't wait; he was using his spurs, thundering out of the yard and away.

Cooler now, Seldon came to his feet and headed back into the barn. At the door of the harness room, Fay said, "Brad? It's you! That shot—?"

"He's gone," Seldon said and found the knife again and went to work on the ropes of the others. When he'd freed them all and they'd finished chafing their wrists and stamping circulation into their legs, Seldon jerked the dangling hangrope from the rafter hook and hefted the coiled hemp.

"It's real enough," he said. "If it wasn't for this, I'd still think I'd dreamed the whole thing."

"That gent was no dream!" Wheeler protested. "What did you do—break the rope at your wrists? You must have given him a surprise when you showed fight. Wonder if he thought we were all free, and if that was what stampeded him? For a minute I wasn't too sure what was really going on myself."

"His way has been to knock his victims unconscious and hang them afterward," Fay said scornfully. "He thought Brad was as good as unconscious, with his wrists and ankles tied. He lost his nerve when he found things were different."

Wheeler said, "We could get ourselves horses and cut sign on him, but there's more important work to do. I've got to get back across the Trinity before it's too late. Maybe the Pool's already riding to look for me."

Excitement put a high pitch to Seldon's voice. "You think they might come?"

"When I first saw the signal fire on the island, I was a little suspicious," Wheeler said. "It was the old sign Fay and I used, and I supposed she had some reason for not wanting to come back to the Wagonwheel. I decided to go for a look, but some of the other homesteaders were afraid it might be a trap. I told them to come riding if I wasn't back in a reasonable time."

"God!" Seldon ejaculated. "And Munger's men are strung out along the river just hoping the Pool will come!

Don't you see? If the homesteaders set foot on S-5's land, Munger's got all the excuse he needs to start shooting. We'd better be riding!"

They came out of the barn together; a heavy silence held the ranch and every building was dark and deserted, even Ki's cook-shack. Crossing the yard, they came upon Shep; the little collie lay stretched upon the ground, a limp bundle of fur, but when Fay bent for a look at the dog, she said, "There's still life in him!"

Banning also knelt to make an examination. "He's been creased along the top of the head—knocked unconscious," he decided. "You know, the way a hunter sometimes creases a wild horse he wants to capture. McSwain was likely shooting to kill, but he was half an inch too high!"

Fay scooped the dog up into her arms with an effort. "Poor old Shep," she said. "I'll see what I can do for him while you fellows are getting the horses."

She went staggering toward the house with her burden; Seldon and Wheeler and Banning headed for the corral, and here Seldon found his own roan saddler and Fay's mount, and they got gear onto two other mounts as well. Banning saddled up silently; and when the task was finished, he stood for a moment, his eyes on Seldon. "We're right back where we were when Munger surprised us in the office this noon," Banning said then. "Do I ride along with you, Seldon?"

Seldon's mind went to that moment when Banning had charged Munger and had been brought to his knees by Singleton's gun barrel. "We could use your gun; I reckon every one will count," Seldon said slowly. "Can I depend on you, Banning?"

S-5's manager said, "Believe me, the only man I'm beholden to tonight is Cholla Sam. You'll be making no mistake, Seldon."

Seldon glanced at Wheeler; the Pool leader lifted his shoulders in an expressionless shrug, and Seldon nodded, and the three led the horses to the ranch house. Lamplight splashed from a window now; and when they trooped inside, they found that Fay had made a bed of blankets for Shep on the floor of her own room; she'd bathed the dog's wound and Shep was lying glassy-eyed and quiet, but he was licking her hand.

She said, "I've done everything I can for him. It should be safe to leave him now. I'll be riding to the Trinity with you."

"We'll need guns," Seldon said.

They found Seldon's own forty-five and gun-belt in Banning's office, and Seldon went then to the cook-shack and quickly sacked up some food. Returning, he found that Banning had rummaged through the house and found weapons for himself and Wheeler. The gun-belts latched on, Seldon said, "You fellers start riding. I want to speak to Fay for a minute. I'll catch up with you."

Fifteen minutes later hoofs rattled as Seldon came at a high gallop to overtake the two who'd walked their horses slowly, waiting for him. Fay was not along, but they could see her in the moonlight, swinging into a saddle back at the ranch-yard gate. Wheeler, studying Seldon's face, said, "You're sending her to town for help? There isn't time to get to Calumet and back before the lid blows off. That's a mighty long ride."

Seldon shrugged. "I sent her on a wild-goose chase, likely," he confessed. "But at least she thinks she's helping, and that makes her willing to go. Now she'll be out of harm's way."

Wheeler nodded. "When there's time, I've got a helluva long apology to make to you," he said.

They lifted their horses to a brisk trot. Seldon shared with the others the food he'd fetched, and they ate as they rode along. Banning looked backward many times, and at last he said, "I can't get McSwain out of my mind. I'm still wondering if one of us maybe shouldn't have gone after him."

"Anybody get a good look at his face?" Seldon asked.

"He had his sombrero tipped low, and there wasn't much light in that harness room," Wheeler said. "All I could see was that he needed a shave, the same as always." His glance strayed to Banning. "Fay told me something the night Boaker was hung, Banning. She'd promised you she'd never mention it, but at the time she thought maybe you were impersonating McSwain, and she had to talk to somebody. She said McSwain hadn't meant the threat he made against you in court."

"The cards have been faced," Banning said. "I've no secrets now. McSwain thought I'd save him from the gallows, and the threat he made against Strawn was a fake, too. But I asked Fay to keep quiet for fear Endicott or Boaker might get to thinking what she thought. If the law had got interested in a tie-up between me and McSwain and started digging for facts, they might have cut sign on the Lampassa Kid."

"Never mind McSwain," Seldon said. "There'll be no real peace in the Hurumpaws till he's run down, but I think I know where I'll find him after this night's work is over."

They soon reached the river, and the moon painted a path across the turbulent water as the Trinity roared into the southeast. Fringing willows made a dark, formless barrier, but there was no sign of men, no sound of conflict. Upon this peacefulness Seldon put an accurate estimate, and he said, "Blue told it that S-5's crew was between the island and Cowper's Ford. We'll have to head south."

In single file they rode silently in that direction, each busy with his own thoughts, Seldon's mind seething with a dozen plans that were discarded as quickly as they were formed. They were three against many; they had no argument to sway S-5's men save the argument of force. A range empire was at stake, and Munger had been made desperate. The issue would have to be faced as it arose; and as they neared the little tear-shaped island, Banning jerked in his saddle, raising a hand for silence; and above the river's strident roar the sound of gunfire reached them.

"It's started!" Banning cried. "Hear those guns? The Pool must be crossing the Trinity!"

"And riding straight into a trap!" Wheeler thundered. "Coming across the river with that wolf pack waiting in the willows to spill them out of their saddles! Let's go!"

But Seldon maneuvered his horse quickly, his hand reaching for Wheeler's bridle and his glance holding the stormy eyes of Wheeler. "Steady!" Seldon advised. "The war's on; there's nothing we can do about that. No sense riding pell-mell against S-5 guns. Our best bet is to hunt out the men like Munger and Singleton and Blue. They're the real leaders of S-5; get them and we've got half the war won. Can you savvy that?"

His voice seemed to steady Wheeler. "You're right," the Pool leader said. "Lead the way, Seldon."

Banning said, "Remember this, both of you. Munger's my bear meat. All mine!"

He wore no hat, his hair was in wild disarray, and his lips were curled back from his teeth in a fighting man's snarl. He was the Lampassa Kid again tonight. He'd been stripped of all spirit once; he'd been used as a pawn and betrayed by the very men who'd used him, but he'd found a new chance for himself. And suddenly Seldon was very glad that Banning was here, and any last doubt about the man was forever dissolved.

But there was no other triumph in Seldon at the moment. He'd come here to stop a range war, and he'd failed, for the war was on; the barking guns along the Trinity gave raucous testimony to that. There was only this left; the war had to be won, and Seldon shuddered at the manifold possibilities that might accrue—saddles emptied and men dying and the homesteaders shoved back across the Trinity, their houses burned, their crops trampled and their fences cut. Such were the things that left scars that never healed, the things that put a bitterness in men that no amount of peaceful living could completely erase. These were the things that there still might be time to prevent.

"Come on!" he said and lifted his mount to a high gallop.

19 ⋮ Wolf Pack Wild

They came racing southward along the river, measuring the need for caution against the need for haste, mindful one moment that the sound of their coming might carry to S-5's hidden men, urged to desperate speed the next moment by the blatant beat of guns. They came abreast of the little island, a dark, bushy vagueness upon the Trinity's heaving breast, for the moon had gone into hiding. Still the fight seemed far away, and they galloped onward another half mile, pausing intermittently to separate sounds from echoes; and as they came to one such stand, Wheeler made the finding that Seldon had suspected and feared.

"They've crossed the river!" Wheeler judged. "Listen hard. Hear those guns now? Over on the other bank! S-5's moved away from us."

Banning said, "You're right, Wheeler. Yet I'll swear the firing was on this side before. That means the Pool started to come over here, probably just below the island; and S-5 opened up on them, drove your friends back to the other bank. Then, while the homesteaders were scattered and cutting for cover, the S-5 must have crossed the Trinity."

Seldon's lips drew to a thin, tight line. "Then let's get over there," he said.

Forcing his horse down through the willows, he urged the mount out into the river. Wheeler and Banning were close behind him; he heard Wheeler suck in his breath sharply; and when Seldon first felt the strong and steady pull of the current, he understood what had given Wheeler that one bad moment. Seldon had never crossed the Trinity except at the island or Cowper's Ford; and he wondered now if it was wise to swim the river here, when back-tracking to the island would mean easy fording. Here the Trinity was a frothing fury; the horse needed strength and the rider needed skill, but Seldon had committed himself to the try.

Glancing over his shoulder when the shore was yards behind, he saw that Wheeler and Banning were into the water. S-5's manager made a bulging shadow over the stream's surface, but Wheeler was harder to see because he had slipped from his saddle and was tailing across.

That gave Seldon his cue; he had crossed every river between Texas and Montana, and they included those Kansas streams whose banks were dotted by the graves of drowned trail drivers of earlier days; but Seldon could learn about the Trinity from Wheeler, who had made his home beside the stream. Unlatching his gun-belt, Seldon hooked it over the saddle horn, then slipped into the stream. Trying for a hold on one of the stirrups, he failed in that, but he got a good grip on the roan's tail; and he kicked his feet to keep afloat as he let the horse haul him.

Men and mounts were being carried steadily down-stream, but they were angling obliquely toward the opposite bank. Lying this low in the water made it impossible for Seldon to see the far shore or to make any accurate gauge of progress. Twice driftwood logs came bobbing out of the north; these shapeless juggernauts of the night narrowly missed him, and always the roar of the river kept its constant pounding in his ears. He had begun to feel the slow ebbing of his strength; he made several tries at touching bottom with his feet; and finally his toes scraped rock, the roan lurched up a dark, shadowy bank, and Seldon was on solid footing.

Wheeler made a landing a few yards above him; Banning's horse got across too, but its saddle was empty, and Seldon, instinctively catching at the mount's trailing reins, felt the thrust of fear. Wheeler shook himself like some great, shaggy dog. "Saw him slip out of his saddle when we were nearly across," he reported. "From the way he kept trying to stay in the kak, I figgered he didn't put too much faith in his swimming."

Those guns were still beating beyond, the sound much fainter now; but Seldon put his mind against that tocsin. "We've got to find him," he said.

Frantically they beat among the willows and the bushes; they scanned the river's heaving surface and wished for more moonlight; and they called Banning's name again and again, their growing anxiety shaking their voices as they worked downstream. They were losing precious time; Seldon cursed his choice of crossings; and the futility of this search was growing upon him when he heard a weak cry above the river's constant voice. Straining his eyes, Seldon saw Banning then; the man was clinging to a rock a dozen yards out in the stream. Seldon went splashing to him, got an arm around Banning, and hauled him to the bank.

"Swept off my horse," Banning panted. "Not much of a swimmer. . . . Managed to reach that rock—and figured I'd stay there till my wind came back." He dug water from his ears, then had a look at his gun.

Wheeler said, "Let's be riding. From the sound of those sixes, I'm thinking the war's moving toward my Wagonwheel."

Seldon climbed into his saddle again. His impulse was to ride hard, to try recapturing the time lost in the crossing; but once the three were out of the willows and into more open country, he had to remember that they might meet up with S-5 men at any time.

And now they were nearing the Wagonwheel, and Ord Wheeler lifted his hand for a halt. His growing worry reflecting in his voice, he said, "I think I've got it sized up now. They've pushed the Pool back to my place, and the homesteaders have forted up at the ranch. Here's where we buy in."

Seldon came out of his saddle, gestured to the others, and led his mount down into the yawning mouth of a draw. The roan hitched to a bush, he said, "We'd better spread out and go Injun fashion. Munger's men are between us and your place, Ord. They won't be expecting anybody to come up from behind. Maybe we can thin them out a little."

Wheeler anchored his horse and started off afoot. "Be seeing you," he called back, low-voiced; and then he hesitated. For too long he'd had his hatred for Banning and his suspicions concerning Seldon to drop his animosity in a minute. But S-5's men waited beyond, a wolf pack gone wild; and there was a certain solemnity to this facing of death that Wheeler probably felt. "Good luck, fellers," he added gruffly, and the darkness claimed him.

Banning held silent. He had almost drowned at the river crossing, but that ordeal had seemingly only served to steel him. He had been out of his element then, but now he had a gun in his hand, and he went off down the draw with all the surety that might have once been the Lampassa Kid's. Seldon, alone now, began carefully stalking toward the gunfire.

At first he only reconnoitered, not anxious to meet with anyone until he'd surveyed the situation; and he was mindful, too, that he might be fair target for homesteader guns as well as S-5's. He wormed across open ground flat on his stomach, he sought the shelter of every bush and rock, and he was glad now that the moon only showed itself intermittently. By this slow appraisal, he gave himself a solid understanding of the situation.

Pool men had indeed forted up inside Wheeler's shack; others were obviously stationed in the various outhouses, for gun flame blossomed from all the buildings. S-5's renegades had apparently fanned out in a wide, broken circle that enclosed the Wagonwheel's buildings to the west, the south, and the north. Gunmen had crawled into a patch of corn not far from Wheeler's shack; they loosed their lead from this rustling cover, then crawled to different spots as retaliating bullets tried to seek them out.

All this Seldon learned, and within a half-hour he found that the bulk of S-5's men were strung out in a shallow, curving coulee that ran within easy six-gun range of the besieged ranch buildings. Sprawled along the coulee's slope, Munger's men kept up a constant, unrelenting fire over the rim. By a careful marking of gun-flashes, Seldon had discovered this; and then, clinging to all possible cover, he maneuvered himself into the coulee and eased along its bottom.

Chokecherry bushes grew here profusely; the going was slow and troublesome, and before he had taken many steps, movement spilled down the slope and the high shape of a man loomed before him. "That you, Ed—?" the fellow said. Seldon laid his gun barrel along the side of the man's head, and as this S-5 rider went down to a long sleep, Seldon said, with a deep satisfaction, "That makes one less, bucko!"

He'd estimated the respective might of the Pool and S-5 on the day the two factions had been in town for Limpy McSwain's hanging. He'd judged then that about twenty-five men called Ord Wheeler leader, while a score rode for S-5. But something more than a difference in numbers had to be taken into account. The homesteaders were of varying ages; many were having their first baptism of gunfire; others were so old that age had dimmed their shooting-eyes; and all of them were trained to the plow and peace. S-5's crew was the gathered outcasts of many ranges, savants of the gun. Long practice in dark ways gave them the fighting edge.

These factors Seldon weighed as he moved along, but that surprise encounter with an S-5 man had sharpened his caution. Thus he became aware that two men were ahead of him before they had any inkling of his presence, and he tested each footfall as he eased forward. One of those men ahead spoke, sharp impatience in his voice. "Why doesn't Poe order a rush, Shag?" he demanded. "We could clean those jiggers out in a hurry."

That was the deep voice of Blue, and Shag Singleton gave him answer. "Munger's got a better notion. When the sign's right, he's going to torch those buildings."

His voice low, Seldon said, "Howdy, boys," and drew a savage satisfaction from the way his words made them jump. But they were all instinct, and their instinct ran true to form. Lifting their guns, they fired at the sound of his voice; but he'd already taken a quick, sideward step, anticipating their reaction. He got Singleton with his first shot; the high figure of the man doubled over and went sprawling. Blue chose then to take to his heels. He went zigzagging up the coulee, and Seldon, shedding caution, ran after him. Blue was shouting hoarsely. "Munger! Munger! Seldon's here! In the coulee!"

Blue's voice blurred as he tripped over some small obstruction and went down heavily. Hitting the ground, Blue rolled, firing back at Seldon; and Seldon, feeling the airlash of a bullet along his cheek, triggered methodically; the feel of the bucking Colt was good against his hand. When he got to Blue, the man was dead; and Seldon stood panting, wondering how far the man's warning had carried above the constant beat of guns, wondering if others would be coming quickly. Someone was moving down the coulee toward him, a vague, shadowy form; and Seldon threw up his gun and stood tense and ready. Thus Gus Banning might have died if he hadn't moved into a patch of feeble moonlight at that moment.

Seldon expelled his breath gustily. "Thought you were Munger," he said. "I just got Blue and Singleton, but I'm afraid the fat's in the fire. Let's get out of here."

Banning gestured toward the coulee's slope. "Don't worry about Munger," he said, his voice brittle. "I just ran into him. I told you he was my meat, Seldon. Have you seen Wheeler?"

Such was Poe Munger's epitaph, an old account was closed, and Seldon wondered how it had been at the last showdown between the Lampassa Kid and the man who had known about the pardon and laughed in Banning's face when the truth had come out. Also, it was Seldon's thought that luck and nerve had carried them far this night. They had known that Singleton and Blue and Munger were the backbone of the renegade bunch; and a few ounces of lead, sprinkled properly, had broken that backbone. Victory was that much nearer, but suddenly Seldon became aware that the guns had gone silent.

"They've quit firing!" he said. "What do you make of that, Banning? S-5 can't be pulling freight?"

Banning shrugged, and a voice rose stridently, farther up the coulee. "Hey, you stubble-jumpers!" it called. "Better toss down your guns and come out with your hands hoisted. We've got your head man here, savvy. And he's a gone gosling if you don't string along!"

Out of the numbing silence that followed, someone shouted from the besieged ranch house. "You're bluffing!"

"Sing out, Wheeler!" the first voice ordered.

Seldon heard Wheeler's hoarse bellow. "Tell 'em to go to hell, boys!" Wheeler shouted. "Sure, they've got me. But that don't mean anything unless you're fools enough to let it!"

"Wheeler!" Seldon gasped and understood everything then, for Wheeler had somehow blundered into S-5's hands and was a hostage once again. Loyalty to Wheeler could be the Pool's undoing in the next few moments; and Seldon began running, charging up the coulee with Banning hard after him. Seldon had no time for planning; he had only a desperate need to get to Wheeler, to try at plucking the man from the midst of his captors. So thinking, he came running to a spot where the coulee broad-

ened, and here he found Wheeler, surrounded by a dozen S-5 hands.

Afterward Seldon was to try to reconstruct that scene, but it would always remain chaotic in his mind. Wheeler was the central figure, of course; the man stood spread-legged and defiant among his enemies, a somber figure against the dark backdrop of the coulee's slope. But the S-5 men were motionless only for a moment; they saw Seldon and Banning coming, and they began firing at once, and this blur of activity brushed all the coherence out of the picture.

Seldon instantly sprawled forward, hugging the ground tightly as lead sleeted above him; and Banning also came down. But Banning had a broken gun-arm now, Seldon heard him curse for a moment, and then Banning got his gun into his left hand and began shooting. Seldon was making his six-gun speak, too; he sensed that this was the finish, and his main concern was to sell himself at a good price.

Then horsemen came charging down the coulee, a dozen of them; and Seldon held his fire, not certain for a moment whether they were other S-5 men or homesteaders who had somehow got into saddles and made a wild rush to Wheeler's rescue. But they were neither. Charlie Fenton led these newcomers, a little man perched upon a horse that could have carried three his size; Dan Courtney rode at Fenton's side; and the others were surveyors also.

They had surprise on their side, these newcomers; they surrounded S-5's men with startling efficiency, and guns were being dropped and hands were hoisting, and there wasn't much to it after that. Seldon got to his feet and lurched forward; mounted surveyors straggled up the coulee, herding S-5 men before them, and Wheeler was shouting orders to the homesteaders who came streaming from cover and down into the coulee. Somewhere in this confusion, Seldon found Fay. She came lurching out of her saddle and into his arms, and he was holding her when Charlie Fenton plucked at his elbow.

"This girl fetched your note, Considine," Fenton said. "Plain gibberish, it was! *There's a fight building up,* you wrote. *Please keep Miss Abbott at your camp till it's over.*"

Fenton's dour face was clean-shaven, Seldon noticed. He said, "She thought I was sending her for help, but that was my way of getting her out of danger. You told me how you stood when it came to mixing into other people's troubles, Fenton. I didn't think there was a chance you'd really come and side us."

"Do you believe everything you hear, you young fool!" Fenton snapped. "If you'd let me miss a show this size, I'd have chased you from here to Mexico. Luckily we finished our survey today, hacked off our whiskers, and started south for Calumet. We met this little lady up by the north bridge, and after we'd talked to her we borrowed horses from one of those homesteader layouts up above. Now I'll be getting along. Confound it, I'm too old a man to be mixing up in such fool melodrama as this!"

Two Pool men passed by, carrying Gus Banning over the hump to Wheeler's shack. Seldon followed after them, his arm around Fay, and surveyors and homesteaders herded disarmed S-5 men into one of the corrals. Inside the shack, Seldon had a look at Banning's arm and found Pool men who had hurts as well. Three homesteaders had died when the Pool tried crossing the Trinity, he learned; a skittish S-5 hand had opened fire too soon and thus the Raggedy Pants men had been given some warning; otherwise the ambush might have netted many lives. Seldon said, "I'm going into Calumet soon. I'll send Doc Budge out here."

Fay had got a fire going in the stove. S-5 lead had made a sieve of the chimney, but she wanted to heat water for the cleansing of wounds; and she put coffee on to boil, also, the smell of it reminding Seldon that it had been a long time since he'd had a warm meal. She looked up quickly, saying, "Do you have to go, Brad?"

Glancing around him, he saw Wheeler talking vociferously to a group of his friends, and he drew a sober delight from the thought that the range war was over and won and that a good and lasting peace had come to the Hurumpaw. Pool men had carried Banning here as an enemy; now they were learning the truth, and they would be caring for Banning as a friend. Even the smell of gunsmoke would soon be gone, but there was a one last chore to do.

"Yes, Fay, I've got to go," Seldon said. "A few S-5 men slipped away from us tonight; they don't matter, but Gary Strawn does. They were only tools, those men we killed or rounded up. Strawn himself is the man I want. There'd be no peace for me if he got away free."

20 ⋮ Flame of a Forty-Five

Somewhere beyond Cowper's Ford, Seldon met Buck Prentiss riding toward S-5's range; it was early morning then, and the new sheriff had half a dozen men with him, townspeople who had taken a neutral stand in the basin's troubles and thereby qualified for posse duty. Seldon was alone. He had slipped away from the Wagonwheel without telling anyone but Fay of his intentions; from his point of view the capture of Strawn was a personal issue. Last night he had welcomed Fenton's help, and he would be forever beholden to the little surveyor for turning the tide of battle. But there'd been many lives at stake, and that made a difference. Today's was a man-to-man affair.

"Morning," Prentiss said when they'd reined up. "What puts you in such a lather?"

"Is Strawn in town, Buck?"

"Couldn't say. I've been mighty busy. The Pool sent me word yesterday afternoon that Easy had been hung and that I'd find him down by the railroad bridge. I fetched him in and had a proper funeral. Oh, you knew about Easy, eh? Then, last night, I had to jug that Chink cook of S-5's; he'd come into town for a load of grub and gotten himself a skinful of laughing water. He tried to tell me something, but he kept mixing up three languages—the son-of-a-gun speaks Mex, too—and it wasn't till his head began shrinking back to size this morning that I savvied the straight of it. Some wild yarn about Munger making prisoners of you and Banning and the Abbott girl and locking you in the barn. That's what fetched me riding."

Seldon said, "Too bad Ki didn't see you when he first hit town. But the big show's all over, Buck. There's nobody at S-5, but you might head for the Wagonwheel. You'll find a passel of prisoners for your jail. Ord Wheeler will spin the yarn for you; me, I'm in a hurry."

He loped on then, and soon he saw a black banner of smoke smearing the southern horizon; the eastbound train had pulled out of Calumet. Shortly thereafter Seldon sighted the town. He came riding along the main street to the courthouse and racked his horse before the rusty building, and the ancient steps echoed to his feet as he hurried upward to Strawn's office. But he found the door locked, and he spent a split-second wondering if Strawn had not yet come to work or if the man was elsewhere in the building. The door to Boaker's chambers stood open, and Seldon found the jurist at his desk.

"Where's Strawn?" Seldon asked.

Boaker swung around in his chair. "Why, hello, Brad," he said. "Say, I'm mighty glad to see you! Buck Prentiss rode out a while ago to pull you out of a jam, but it doesn't look like you need his help. Strawn? He took the morning train for Havre not over half an hour ago. Some sort of legal business. Say, what in thunder's been going on in the basin anyway?"

Disappointment washed through Seldon, leaving him weak; and he cursed the time he'd wasted eating and resting at the Wagonwheel before hitting his saddle again. "Think hard, Judge," he begged, still clinging to a last hope. "How did Strawn act before he left? I've got to know whether it really was business that took him out of town."

"He did act queer," Boaker reflected. "I was standing at yonder window earlier, and I saw Strawn come out of the Elite Café. Two S-5 riders loped into town, a couple of those gunnies that Munger hired. Strawn talked to them, and after they'd ridden on, he came over to the courthouse mighty fast. Babbled something about having to go to Havre, and I walked to his office with him. He practically cleaned out his desk."

"God!" Seldon groaned. "Two S-5 men! A few of them got away from us last night, and Strawn must have pumped them about what happened. A rat's just deserted a sinking ship, Judge. Gary Strawn doesn't intend to come back to Calumet. He's slipped through my fingers for sure. A telegram to the next town might stop him, but likely he'll jump train on the other side of the Hurumpaws just to be safe. He's gone—gone—"

Boaker, his brows puckered, said, "I wish you'd tell me what you're driving at, boy. If—"

But Seldon, stiffening as a new thought struck him, was striding to the window and glancing out toward the depot and the sun-burnished rails that stretched from Calumet to the far horizon. He'd followed that railroad track into Calumet when he'd first come to the basin, and it was easy to reverse that trip in his mind and to trace Gary Strawn's flight. The railroad ran due east from here, crossing the Trinity over the bridge from which Easy Endicott had been hanged; and then, beyond the river, the rails swung north, paralleling the Hurumpaw Hills for many miles and then swinging again for the climb.

No horse alive could overtake a train half an hour gone. Not on a straight stretch. But hard riding might bring a man *across* country to the Hurumpaws and to the tracks ahead of the train. Riding directly northeast by way of Cowper's Ford would be taking a shortcut that would lop miles from the route followed by the train. It was worth a try, and the thought, growing upon Seldon, filled him with hope.

"Judge!" he cried. "I'm going after Strawn! Never mind how or why. I'll tell you all about it later. Find Doc Budge for me, will you? Tell him he's needed at the Wagonwheel. I'll be seeing you!"

Then he was running for the stairway and taking it in a series of leaps, and he came out to the hitchrack and got his roan saddler. Here was a horse that had done much hard and faithful traveling in the past hours, and he led the mount to the livery stable and dragged the hostler from his chair. "Stable this jughead for me, friend," Seldon ordered. "And pile gear on the fastest, freshest cayuse you've got. Hurry, man!"

He did most of the saddling himself; impatience made his fingers wooden, but he went out of Calumet a few minutes later at a high gallop, his long body bent over the saddle horn. He had covered this trail many times, but he had never ridden it like this. He didn't spare himself or the mount; he raced across the tangled terrain between the town and the ford with a reckless disregard for any consequences, using all of a lifetime's riding lore to put the miles behind him, slithering down the slopes of coulees he'd once skirted and humping up the higher rises.

He'd got a good horse, but he needed one with wings today; and when Seldon came again to Cowper's Ford, the sun stood much higher than he'd hoped it would. Across the river, he was onto Raggedy Pants holdings, covering much of the same route he and Munger had followed the day they'd headed into the high Hurumpaws to take Charlie Fenton off a train. The scenery blurred past him, the taste of the wind was in his mouth, but the horse was beginning to falter. Now there were fences to slow Seldon. A fresher horse might have jumped some of them. Seldon marked the curling smoke of a ranch house and headed for it. The place belonged to one of the Pool men who'd been at the besieged Wagonwheel, but the man had since returned to his family, and he came out into the yard and listened to Seldon's request.

"A fresh horse," Seldon pleaded. "Never mind the questions now, mister. I've got to get to the hills ahead of the train. Gary Strawn's on it."

"Strawn?" The homesteader's interest quickened. "Mister, I'll get you a horse that's a cross between quicksilver and a bolt of buttered lightning. Wheeler and Banning did a lot of talking to us boys before we headed home. So Strawn cut and run!"

"I'll fetch him back," Seldon promised.

Soon he was onto a fresh horse and away, and now he could take the fences by a simple lift on the reins. Time rushed to the steady thudding of hoofs; the hills loomed closer; they were beginning to bulk above him; and he knew the railroad couldn't be far away. But he'd lost all sense of time and distance in this frantic race against those very things, and he wondered if the train had already passed this point. Time and again he strained, trying to catch the roar of the locomotive, but the wind was in his ears and the beating hoofs made ceaseless thunder.

He began wondering then if there'd be a second chance to overtake the train if he reached the track too late. He drew on his memory for a picture of the railroad from here on to the east, and he recalled that the track climbed upward to the Hurumpaw water tank, then started down the far slope. There was a tunnel beyond, he remembered, and after that a high trestle over a deep gulch. His mind went no farther than that, for he was sick with the realization that he couldn't lop off more miles if the train had already passed this point.

Then he reached the track, but here it curved up into the hills; timber flanked the embankment, and he could see no more than a quarter of a mile in either direction along the track. Flinging himself from the saddle, he put one ear to a rail; and the steel was trembling. He could hear the train now; its smoke bannered faintly above distant tree tops. He'd beaten it here, and he got into the saddle again, his heart pounding and a fierce and savage joy surging through him.

This horse, too, had done about all the running it could do for one day; he leaned and patted the cayuse's neck and said, "Good boy! Good boy!" Then the train came roaring into sight, a locomotive hauling a baggage car and a single coach with an observation platform behind. The cars thundered past him; he spurred along the embankment, asking this one last effort from the horse; and he got a hold on the observation platform's railing, kicked his feet free of the stirrups, and hauled himself aboard.

For a moment he stood here, watching the widening distance drop the horse behind. Seldon was trembling from the effort of this long ride, and he wanted control of himself before he entered the coach. The train swung around the curve, the horse was gone from sight—had probably already turned back toward its home corral—and the engine started its slow climb up into the Hurumpaws.

Rested, Seldon fumbled with the door and came into the rear of the coach. There were only a few passengers, he noticed, but one of them was Gary Strawn. The man was near the end of the coach, and he was using two seats; he'd thrown back one and now had his long legs stretched out upon it; but there was still room for a man to sit, and Seldon came up the aisle and slipped into the seat, facing Strawn.

"Howdy," Seldon said.

Strawn was hunched down into the cushions, his hat pulled low over his eyes; and Seldon knew then, by the man's jerk of surprise, that Strawn had been dozing and hadn't seen him as he'd ridden alongside the train before quitting his saddle. Strawn said, "Seldon? Where the devil did you come from?"

"That doesn't matter, Strawn. I'm here. And I'm taking you back to Calumet, mister."

"Taking me back? For Pete's sake, why?"

Seldon took his own time answering. He watched the banked timber march past them, and then he said, "For two reasons. First, because you were the man behind Munger and Singleton and Blue and all the small fry that did the dirty work in the basin. They're all dead, Strawn; or maybe you found that out this morning."

He spoke of the ambush at the Trinity and the war at

the Wagonwheel, drawing a full picture, and when it was finished, he said, "The Hurumpaw is going to be a nice, neighborly place to live, from here on out; but that doesn't quite satisfy me. It would keep getting between me and an honest night's sleep, if you went free. But that isn't all. You lost this hand, Strawn, so you're running. But there are other Mungers and Blues and Singletons. You'd draw men like them to you, and you'd give some other range trouble. That's not going to happen."

Strawn had listened silently; now he carefully put his feet to the floor, and his lips drew tight. "Just what is it you think you know?"

"Nearly everything. I know that Banning was the Lampassa Kid and that you had a tight hold on him. I know what you intended doing in the basin—and how near you came to doing it. That's all over, Strawn. You weren't around when the big fight came off, of course. No, you headed into Calumet and stayed there. That's the way of your kind, feller. Somebody else does the dying. The only time you ever dirtied your hands was when it was good and safe. Like when you were impersonating Limpy McSwain, for instance."

Strawn said, oddly, "Care for a cigar?" and he reached toward the inner breast pocket of his coat. But Seldon's hand moved faster; he got a grip on Strawn's wrist, and with his free hand Seldon plucked a forty-five from a shoulder holster Strawn wore. The play was made quickly; they'd kept their voices to an ordinary pitch; and the other passengers were unaware of all this.

Seldon said, "That was your last bluff, Strawn, and it didn't work. You *were* playing Limpy, weren't you?"

Strawn was done with pretense; his lip curled back from his teeth, and he said, "Go to hell! Do you think I'm fool enough to admit anything?"

"You don't have to. I knew last night it was you masquerading as Limpy. In the first place, you came directly to the harness room out at S-5—which proves you knew you'd find me there. That meant you'd seen Munger, and he'd told you where I was hogtied. But it was Shep, the collie, who really called your brand. He began growling when you rode up. Fay Abbott once told me that the dog didn't take to you; that didn't seem important at the time, but last night it made sense."

Strawn glanced out of the window and held to a surly silence for a long time. Then: "You couldn't prove a thing in a court of law," he said. "Do you think I haven't considered that angle?"

"From the first, I figured that somebody was impersonating Limpy," Seldon said. "McSwain was dead; I had Buck Prentiss's word for that. And I'd learned how easy it was to put over an impersonation. People actually remember others by their personalities, not by their faces, and personality is made of many things—a mannerism, a way of dressing, for instance. All I had to do to pretend to be Hush Considine was to wear black garb, keep my throat covered, and talk in a whisper. Any man of Limpy's lanky build could pass for him just as easy. That limp made him a marked man; the blue shirt and old levis were easily duplicated. You have a mustache, and the beard stubble could have been made by smearing lampblack or grease, or anything that could be washed off afterward. You always rode by night; so nobody ever got a close look at you. And you even kept the truth from Munger and your own bunch, making sure your secret stayed a secret."

Strawn said, "You've still proved nothing. What about a motive?"

"That's simple. You wanted the law of Hurumpaw out of the way; honest lawmen stood between you and your scheme. If you'd put Munger or his gunnies to shooting men like Boaker and Endicott, you'd have set S-5 on the wrong side of the fence and maybe had the governor investigating. But you sat in court and heard McSwain threaten the very men you wanted dead; and what's more, he threatened you, too, and Banning, though that was only bluff. It seemed a safe proposition to go riding as Limpy and to carry out Limpy's threat. After all, folks thought *you* were on Limpy's list. By the way, what did you do with Limpy's body?"

He expected no answer, but, surprisingly, Strawn said, "I moved it the very first night. No, I'm not saying where I buried him after that. You see, I'll deny all this in court. But I thought that some fool would open the grave the first time Limpy appeared to be riding. But Endicott was too sure Limpy was really dead, though eventually Easy cracked and had to have his look."

"Speaking of Endicott, you must have ridden after him while I was trying to carve my way out of jail. But why did you bother with him, Strawn? After all, he'd turned in his badge and was leaving the basin."

"Endicott would have come back," Strawn said. "He was stampeded for the moment, but he had guts, and he'd have come back."

"You're a thorough scoundrel," Seldon said. "The night you hanged Boaker, I suppose you intended showing yourself as McSwain afterward, but that wasn't necessary since Fay Abbott saw you. So you changed to your own clothes, cleaned your face, and showed up to help her pack Boaker to the doctor."

Strawn peered from the window; the train was passing the water tank, but it didn't pause here; the hard pull was up the opposite slope of the Hurumpaws. Strawn said, "I came back because I wanted to know why she was visiting Boaker in the middle of the night. I'd always had my suspicions about her; Munger had told me of her meetings with Wheeler on the island. I wanted Banning to get rid of her long ago; but when it came to her, Banning would only stand so much pushing."

"A nice game while it lasted, Strawn. How would it have ended? I suppose Limpy McSwain would have just disappeared, and folks could have gone on forever looking for him without cutting sign."

"You've pieced it together pretty well, Seldon," Strawn said and peered from the window again. The train was rolling downhill and braking against the grade. "Yes, I wanted the law out of the way, and I thought I'd found a means of stampeding them. I counted on Greenleaf and Prentiss getting scared out after Boaker was hanged. Greenleaf was mighty afraid, but he stayed, poor fool. Prentiss was next on my list."

"And me," Seldon said. "You wanted me dead, too; and since I'd helped hang Limpy, I qualified for the list."

"Exactly," Strawn admitted. "Yes, I did see Munger yesterday, just as you guessed. He told me he had you prisoner and was going to grab Wheeler and draw the Pool across the Trinity. Munger thought you'd make a good hostage, but I reasoned that if you were dead there'd be no chance of your getting away to interfere at the showdown. I was going to hang Banning, too; Munger told me Gus had learned of the pardon and turned against us. I'd have left Wheeler and the girl alive to tell Cholla Sam Seldon that Limpy McSwain had got you, when Cholla Sam came running, as he'd have been bound to do when the news reached him."

"That puts the last piece into the puzzle," Seldon said. "We'll be getting off at the first stop, Strawn, and catching us a train back to Calumet tonight. You know your law, and you'll deny everything you've told me, I reckon, but I think any Hurumpaw jury will hear me out and hang you. You'll stretch a new rope, Strawn, and there'll be irony in that. For you'll be getting just what Limpy McSwain told you you'd get!"

"I wonder," Strawn said and craned for a look out the window again.

And then, suddenly, this coach was utterly dark, and Seldon realized, too late, what Strawn had been watching for. The railroad tunnel on this slope of the Hurumpaws! Seldon had heard the train whistle for the tunnel, but the sound hadn't registered upon his consciousness; he'd been

too intent upon his talk with Strawn. And he knew now
why Strawn had made partial confession; the man had
been attempting to lull him, bargaining for time for the
train to reach this tunnel.

Strawn had planned well, and Strawn carried another
gun besides the one Seldon had plucked from the shoulder
holster. For the impenetrable darkness of the tunnel was
broken by the flame of a forty-five in the hand of Gary
Strawn, and Seldon was thrust back hard against the seat
by the smashing impact of the slug.

21 ⋮ The Hills of Home

Seldon lurched sideways, his move instinctive, the moment he had sensed Strawn's intention; and thus the bullet that might have split Seldon's heart smashed along his ribs. At first the pain and shock almost swept him into a greater darkness, but he fought for a tight hold on himself, and he struck out with his fist at the man across from him. All this happened swiftly; Strawn was already gone, lurching out into the aisle and along it toward the end of the coach. Seldon went stumbling after him, praying for sustaining strength; he got his fingers on Strawn's coat and tried hard for a good hold, but Strawn escaped him.

Seldon thought, *I can't let him get away!* and he held to that thought as he might have held to a tangible support. He knew that if Strawn managed to jump train, these high hills would shelter the man from any posse; and though Strawn would be forever outlawed, there was always another name and another range. Seldon felt the draft as the rear door was pulled open. He careened through it after Strawn, choked and gasped as the engine's smoke enfolded him; and then as the train came out of the tunnel, Strawn assumed shape and substance like a released genie, and Seldon grappled with the man on the little observation platform.

Strawn still held that second gun in his hand, but Seldon got a tight grip on Strawn's wrist, and he fought to keep Strawn from triggering effectively or using the gun as a club, fought with all of his waning strength, pitting himself against the wiriness that had enabled Strawn to handle such bulky men as Endicott and Boaker. Passengers were coming down the aisle; if they hadn't heard the report of the gun above the rumbling of the train through the tunnel, some of them must have seen the gun flash. Strawn, his face twisted into a grotesque mask by hard straining, managed to lower his gun-arm a little; and he fired again. A star-shaped hole blossomed in the glass of the door leading from the coach, and the passengers fell back with a noticeable loss of enthusiasm for any part of this fight.

Seldon's side was sticky with blood, and he was sure one of his ribs was broken. Vertigo made a myriad squirming Strawns out of the one he battled; he knew that he must conquer Strawn quickly or not at all. The train was rolling along a low embankment, the engine was still braked against the grade, and this would make a good place for Strawn to jump, once he freed himself. Trying all the while to keep Strawn's arms pinioned, Seldon suddenly adopted a new tactic. Releasing Strawn, Seldon fell back a pace and swung his right fist at Strawn's jaw, a hard, calculated blow that took the edge from the last reserve of Seldon's strength.

He missed, his knuckles grazing Strawn's shoulder, and Strawn got in another shot then; the bullet laid its fire along Seldon's hip, and he thought that his left leg was going to buckle. He struck out once more, struck wildly, blindly, and this time his knuckles cracked against Strawn's chin. Strawn went back hard against the platform's railing; he fought for balance, his arms flailing, and then he somersaulted backward over the railing and was gone.

Managing a tottering step forward, Seldon reached the railing and had a look. He expected to see Strawn sprawled along the embankment, and bitterness surged through Seldon, for this was not the way he'd planned. He'd hoped to put Strawn out of the fight; instead he'd knocked Strawn from the train, and if the man had suffered no broken bones in the fall, then Strawn had accomplished the very purpose for which he'd fought.

Then Seldon saw Strawn, and he raised his arm before his eyes to shut off the horror of that sight.

The train had reached the trestle, that high, spider-legged trestle that crossed a wide canyon below the tunnel; the coach was rumbling over that deep gorge with the tiny, winding creek far, far below. And Strawn was falling, turning over and over in the air, a shapeless twisting thing of flailing arms and legs, going to his death on those jagged rocks that awaited him—going to meet a stern sort of justice beyond any book or law.

Seldon stumbled back into the coach then; the passengers came crowding up to steady him, their voices blending into a confused babble in his ears. He saw the conductor coming down the aisle, a bulking bigness of blue serge and brass buttons. He put his hand out toward the man, seeing the conductor as a steady rock to sustain him. The darkness came crowding upon him; the aisle swooped upward to strike him in the face; he went spinning down, feeling faint and disembodied and beyond all power to help himself; and he knew then how it had been for Strawn in the last, awful moment.

There came a day when Doc Budge grudgingly consented to allow his most recalcitrant patient out of bed, and thus, after the pudgy little medico had taken himself off toward Calumet town, Brad Seldon pulled on his pants, shrugged into a shirt, and tottered over to the bureau in this little bedroom at S-5 and had a look at his wan reflection in the mirror.

He had lain here these several weeks, he had learned to know every detail of this room, and he had come to like it, even though he'd chafed under the inactivity of the sickbed and laid several preposterous claims to strength, while Doc Budge had regarded him with a fishy and unenthusiastic eye. But a man had to get riding sometime, and Seldon crossed over to the window and had a look at the corral where his own roan saddler, fetched from Calumet's livery stable, stomped impatiently. A trail was calling, and now that the hour neared when he might answer that call, he wondered why it had lost a good part of its lure for him.

He'd made friends here in the Hurumpaws, he reflected, and there'd been a parade of them through this bedroom to pay their respects. Judge Boaker and Sheriff Buck Prentiss had spent spare hours here. Ord Wheeler and other Raggedy Pants Pool men had sat by the bed, fumbling with their sombreros and hard put for words, still finding themselves slightly ill at ease on S-5 land, habit being a hard taskmaster. Ki had filled him with strengthening broths, and Fay had constantly fussed over him. Charlie Fenton and his surveyors had called upon him, too, paying a last visit just the other day. They were gone now; some other range needed measuring, and a man went where his work took him.

That was it—that was the thing that made a difference; he had put a Ranger's badge away to do another job; and now the badge had lost some of its luster. There was no accounting for that, and he stood looking out into S-5's sun-drenched yard and wondering; and Shep, fully recovered from Strawn's bullet, went padding off toward the barn.

"Hi, old boy," Seldon said softly.

He could catch an oblique glimpse of the Hurumpaws, and he lifted his eyes to those cool blue heights, and he said, in the old familiar whisper, "The hills of home. The hills of home." He wondered how he had come by that phrase, whether it was something he had read in the past, or words he had wrought in delirium and still held to. They were good on the tongue, and he liked them. And if Hurumpaw Basin had been strange to him when he'd come to Calumet, all that had changed since. This was Montana, and Montana was home.

Someone was knocking at the bedroom door; he knew that knock; he had learned to identify it even in the fever that had attended his first hours here after he'd been fetched back from the far slope of the Hurumpaws by the train's conductor. He said, "Come in," and Fay entered. She stood looking at him in astonishment; she had obviously expected he'd be in bed.

"Doctor's orders?" she asked.

He smiled. "I wore Budge down, like rain wears away a rock."

"You've lost weight," she said irrelevantly.

It came to him that nothing ever dimmed her beauty. She was practically the manager of S-5 for the time being; Gus Banning had gone back to Texas, gone to settle his account with Texas law and to collect the pardon that had awaited him all these years. A new crew rode S-5 saddlers now, a crew made up of drifting cowboys and old hands summoned from exile and riders from the Raggedy Pants Pool who'd offered to help till others could take their place. Yet with all her myriad duties, Fay had found time for him; and he was grateful.

She said, "What now, Brad?"

He shrugged, and she said, hastily, "I've had a letter from Cholla Sam. He'll be here in a week or two; his broken leg's about mended and he gets around nicely now. You figure on riding away, don't you, Brad? I've seen it in your eyes. But surely you'll wait for him."

"I don't think so," he said. "He'll be wanting to give me a ranch. He always has."

"He said as much," she admitted. "He'd like you to take over S-5; he's buying a new ranch in the Bitter Root, and he intends having Gus Banning run it when Gus gets back from Texas with his slate cleaned. I wrote Cholla Sam about Gus, just the way you asked me to, Brad. He agrees that Gus, in the end, earned himself another chance."

"Sam can find a manager for S-5, too," Seldon said. "I can't lean on him, Fay. I did that for too many years."

She said, "Hasn't it ever occurred to you that it might be the other way around, Brad? Cholla Sam's an old man now; it's him that needs to lean on you."

He read a meaning behind her breathless urgency, and at first it astounded him, and then it left him humble. "Are you just thinking about Cholla Sam, Fay?" he asked.

She colored, but her eyes lost none of their warmth. "I even liked Hush Considine a little bit," she said.

"And *I* thought it was all one-sided!" he said. "Fay, are you sure—very sure?" Her eyes gave him his answer, and he said, "I'll have to send in my resignation to the Rangers."

"No, Brad. I already did that for you. The name and address of your captain was in that letter you got from him about Banning. It's over there in the bureau drawer. I just signed your name to the letter I sent."

With a great show of severity, he said, "Don't you know it's against the law to sign someone else's name to a letter?"

She laughed. "And just what can you do about *that*, mister? You're not a lawman anymore!"

He knew then what he wanted and why he wanted it, and he knew that here was the greatest reward that any man could find at trail's ending. Some day he'd tell her how it was with him, but there was a time for talking and a time for keeping silent; he'd learned that long ago. He could still see the Hurumpaws from where he stood; above one balding crest an eagle soared in free and tireless circles. Seldon reached, his arms enfolding Fay, and he held her close for a long and lingering kiss, and in the midst of it he found time for the thought that it was good to be home to stay.